CW00503972

THE RUNNER
AND
THE ROBBER

By Robert Sells
Martin Sisters Publishing

Published by
Martin Sisters Publishing, LLC
www.martinsisterspublishing.com
Copyright © 2013 Robert Sells
The unauthorized reproduction or distribution of this copyrighted work is
illegal. Criminal copyright infringement, including infringement without by
monetary gain, is investigated by the Federal Bureau of Investigation and is
punishable by up to 5 (five) years in federal prison and a fine of $250,000.
Names, characters and incidents depicted in this book are products of the
author's imagination or are used fictitiously. Any resemblance to actual events,
locales, organizations, or persons, living or dead, is entirely coincidental and
beyond the intent of the author or publisher.
No part of this book may be reproduced or transmitted in any form or by any
means, electronic or mechanical, including photocopying, recording, or by any
information storage and retrieval system, without permission in writing from
the publisher.
All rights reserved. Published in the United States
by Martin Sisters Publishing, LLC, Kentucky.
ISBN: 978-1-62553-077-6
Mystery/Thriller
Cover design by Wendy Bublaugh
Edited by Kathleen Papajohn
Printed in the United States of America
Martin Sisters Publishing, LLC

DEDICATION

For my father, Duke Sells, whose golden years were blackened by Alzheimer's.

ACKNOWLEDGEMENTS

I must first acknowledge a former student, Carlena DiSalvo. When she thumbed through my first book, she balked at reading it. "It's so long and the words are so hard." So, this book flows more quickly and is clear while being concise. My daughter Caressa, far closer to young adult realm than her doddering father, gave some helpful insights about what the younger generation was thinking. She edited the early version of the book and got me on the right track with the characters. My editor, Elizabeth Hardy, polished my writing with many suggestions about the art of writing. One of the last edits was done by Karen Weidman. Her suggestions were astute. The dedication and sharp eye of Kathleen Papajohn, the editor for Martin Sisters, gave the novel a professional edge. The book is better for the combined efforts of all of the above. Two of my physics students, Christina Olverd and Ken Howe volunteered for playing the role of Sarah and Billy on the book cover. Conaroga is a combination of three villages in western New York: Dansville, Geneseo, and Mt. Morris. It is also the home of Gus LeGarde, the reluctant mystery sleuth in the Aaron Lazar's novels. Great reads, interesting plots, I urge you to read one or more of Lazar's novels. Finally, as ever, my wife was a patient confidant and a reliable reader. If she finds it interesting, most others will as well. I kept tweaking the novel until she found it interesting.

CHAPTER ONE

Old Tom struggled with the gear shift, a grinding sound announced success and the school bus jerked forward. He was called "Old" because his head is crowned with wavy, pure white hair. His smooth face attested that he was probably not much older than my mom. While the driver and the bus fought, one grumbling loudly and the other answering with loud backfires, the village receded in the back window.

I shifted my view from the driver to the side window I leaned against. The sky was gray. Nothing new there. Last night's wind and rain left the first victims of autumn on the ground: large yellow and green leaves littered roads and yards. All very ugly. I zippered my light jacket up to my throat. It was cold. Again. In Florida right now, it would be sunny and warm.

Old Tom pumped the brakes and the bus eased to the side. I walked to the front, one other passenger, a junior high kid, had already bounced down the steps. Tom smiled when I reached the door. "Way this junk heap is going, you might get home before I climb that hill."

"Don't worry, Jerry will slow me down."

Jerry Smith, an eighth grader, leaned back into the door and impatiently waved for me for me to hurry.

I rolled my eyes and Tom laughed. As soon as I jumped down, Jerry began talking.

"You gonna run again, Bill? You're always running. Gonna run now?"

I hoisted my book bag over my shoulders and tightened the straps a bit. "Yup. Every day, buddy."

"Except when it rains, right? You let Tom drive you last week, huh? Because it was raining."

I shook my head.

"Seems it's always raining here, Jerry. But, yeah, when it rains hard, I take the bus home."

"You just wait when the snow comes. You won't be running then. Sometimes he can't make it up the hill. But, you could stay with me, Bill. We could play my new X-box and…"

"Yeah, we'll see," I said slowly.

His mouth opened again, so I quickly cut him off.

"Gotta go now. Take it easy."

I didn't wait for a response; with Jerry a goodbye could take ten minutes. I started with a slow jog, loosening up. A hundred yards in front of me, I saw the yellow bus loudly protesting the climb up the slight hill. Maybe I would beat Old Tom and the bus to the house. When the sharp wind hit my face the adrenaline began pumping, and I picked up my speed.

I loved to run. Last year I ran varsity for the track team at South Kissimmee High School in Florida. I was the only sophomore on the team. Back then I was just 5 feet, 8 inches tall. Now I was 5 feet, 11 inches. I might even get taller since my Dad was over six feet. My stride was longer than last year and I was faster. Coach was pretty sure I would have qualified for the State's this year. But, last year in Florida wasn't the same as this year in New York. I wouldn't be running for the much smaller, rural school of Conaroga. I picked up my speed and tried to outrace my anger.

When you nearly sprint up a hill, you fight both gravity and fatigue. My body became heavier with every step. As I thought about how unfair life was, I welcomed the fire burning in my leg muscles. I wanted pain now. Pain to match the simmering rage. Why did Dad die and my stupid grandfather have to be alive?

Finally up the hill, I easily maintained the same pace along the plateau that led to Granddad's driveway about a mile away. I could just make out the log cabin Mom now called home.

It wasn't home to me, though. My home was in Florida where my all my friends were. It was Monday and right now a bunch of them would be pouring into the cool of the Florida Mall, getting out of hot sunshine. They would snag some shakes at Johnny Rocket's and hang out with some girls from our school. Every Monday. So, what was I doing in Conaroga this afternoon? After this miserable two mile run, I would shower and hang out with my grandfather. Whoopee! What about Tuesday in Conaroga (when my friends in Orlando were getting geared up for the weekly paintball contest)? After my 'run,' I would shower and hang out with Gramps. Again. And again. And again. Thinking about what I was missing, my frustration grew. Though breathing too hard for this part of the trek, I ran even faster.

A curl of black smoke rose from the cabin's stone chimney. Gramps had built the house himself. His 'larning' had come from doing this or that, not books. He had been a cowboy, a real cowboy, when he was young. In Texas. When his "rump got too damn sore," Granddad had become a logger in Canada. He met my grandmother in a small village deep inside the great forest with "pines trees so close together, you had to slip sideways between them." Grandma decided logging was too dangerous, so early in their marriage they moved to western New York where Gramps became a park ranger at a nearby state park. He stayed on even after she died about ten years ago.

The park was across a narrow gorge, less than a mile away. But getting to the park was a twenty minute car ride over a bridge about five miles north of us. Nothing works right in New York. You can't even travel in straight lines to a park.

Gramps boasted he never had "no gas heater" and he cut his own wood to feed the old black stove in the corner of the living room. The heat from it warmed you like a great, thick quilt you could snuggle into. When I was young, I used to love coming to the cabin. Now that I was the one cutting the wood for the stove I didn't love it as much.

A hundred yards more and I was about to finish with my sprint when I heard a car rumbling behind me. I looked over my shoulder just in time to veer off toward the ditch as the car passed close, too close. The dark green Pontiac trimmed with brown rust swerved in front of me and blocked my path. A tall, thin man, muscles like thick wires, jumped out. He had a salt-and-pepper goatee and wore a wife-beater T-shirt. Up close his pupils were like pin points and angry. The guy grabbed me by my collar and threw me against the trunk of his car.

"Tell your grandfather he damn well better give up some of that money. I want my cut and I'm coming to get it."

With a vise-like grip on my arms, he jammed me against the car a couple of times as though that might help me remember his words better. Before I even thought about defending myself, he tossed me to the ground.

"You understand?"

No, I didn't understand at all, but I figured this was not the best time to ask for an explanation. I vigorously shook my head up and down. He opened the door which protested with a screeching sound, then slammed it shut. Goatee man quickly revved the car so that it seemed to be perpetually exploding and burned rubber as he drove away.

I stayed on the ground, unable to move. I had to remind myself to breathe. I inventoried my body after I got up. A few bruises, but otherwise fine. No sprint now, I simply jogged home wondering what had just happened. Gramps had no money. That much I definitely knew. So, what was Goatee-Man talking about?

Before I opened the door to the cabin I looked back over my shoulder. I heard the muffled engine far away but thankfully not in sight.

I reached for the door handle when the door swung open, banging me against the porch railing. Dressed in a light green uniform, Mom looked at me while she shut the screen door behind her.

"I'm late for work, Billy. Dinner's in the crockpot." She paused for a moment at the door and looked back into the main room. Time stopped for Mom and she smiled at the flannel-shirted figure hunched over the table, his back to us. Then she was gone.

"Bye," I muttered to the car flying out of the driveway.

I stepped inside to a warm house and walked over to the table where an old man's arms rested. A worn baseball hat crowned a nearly bald head. "Hi Gramps."

His attention was riveted to the piles of coins on the table. A long, boney finger carefully slid a nickel from one pile to another. There was a small tower of nickels in one corner of the table while a roughly equal number of quarters rested neatly at the other corner. When he looked up at me, a great smile filled the heavily lined face, the product of a lifetime of smoking. "Hi, Johnny. Good day at the mine?"

"Yeah, Pop. Good day. Go back to your work."

Johnny was my dad's name. My granddad has Alzheimer's and he doesn't always know me. With the way my life had been recently screwed up, I wished I never knew him.

CHAPTER TWO

My dad died nearly two years ago. Cancer. I watched him shrink from this tall, muscular man into a shriveled, trembling bag of bones in less than a year. His treatments and then the drugs needed to ease his pain, sucked all the money out of the bank and left Mom owing over a hundred thousand dollars to Centennial Hospital in Florida. The actual price tag was much more. She used to work there and all the doctors and the nurses declined billing her. She still tears up when she writes a check to pay off our debt. Whether it's for Dad or the kindness showed by the staff, I don't know.

When Dad died, something died inside of Gramps as well. His memory problems got much worse overnight. Last May he was found wandering along the road one rainy night. New York State figured he'd be safer in a nursing home. Maybe they were right, but Mom didn't think so.

We arrived at the nursing home a week later. I was impressed with the manicured gardens in front of the building. The foyer maintained the image of beauty, peace, and care. But, once inside the patient wing, it morphed into something dark and unclean. Patients in worn pajamas aimlessly shuffled about while the one or two aides yawned behind counters. Moaning sounds escaped from under tightly closed doors. Two patients were strapped down in the middle of a hallway, straining to be free, grunts and groans accompanying their futile efforts.

When we reached Granddad's second story room, we saw him looking out the window at pipes and vents. For a man who lived his entire life outdoors, this was the highest order of deprivation. He turned from the window and saw us. The old man in a disheveled hospital gown shuffled to Mom like a little boy who had been hurt and needed a hug.

"Please let me go home, Abby. Please." Mom wrapped her arms around him and, over his shoulder, surveyed the room. The bed wasn't made. In fact, the top sheet was on the floor along with discarded wrappers of all sorts from syringe casings to a crumpled Subway bag. I noticed what looked like some sort of mess under the bed. Vomit? Or... I shook my head. Mom saw it too.

She kissed him on the forehead.

"Stay here for just a little longer." She tried to pull away. Gramps was old, but his grip was iron strong; he held on to her arm like it was a life preserver in a hurricane. Mom gently pried his hand away.

"Don't worry. We'll be back." She patted him on the cheek and he let go.

Mom marched out the door, a wave of her head demanded that I follow. We ended up outside the office of Dr. J. P. Henry, chief administrator of the facility. Though no one entered or left his office, we waited for over an hour. When finally ushered in by the secretary, Mom refused the proffered seat and stood facing him with her arms crossed. Dr. J. P. Henry offered pleasantries; Mom answered with cold stares. Annoyed by her silence, he merely closed his eyes, shook his head which boasted a perfectly groomed beard. After his eyes opened, he ignored Mom and looked at a single paper on his neat mahogany desk.

All the while he tapped the desk repeatedly with his fountain pen. Mom finally spoke.

"We will take care of him. My son and I will move into his home and care for him."

The director of the nursing home stopped tapping and looked across the desk. "Ms. Taylor…"

She scowled at him. "That's Mrs. Taylor."

His eyebrows raised. He looked at his secretary who was taking notes. "Ms. Taylor," he answered with a smug smile, "You don't have power of attorney, and Mr. Taylor is unable to take care of himself. In situations like this…"

"I've listened enough, you money-grabbing bastard, we are his family. All he has left. And, we are going to take him home."

He grabbed the paper in front of him and flicked it in front of Mom.

"This says otherwise, woman."

Mom tilted her head and raised her eyebrows.

"Really?"

"Listen, Ms. Taylor and I suggest you listen well. This paper says Mr. Taylor is under the custody of the state. You have no authority here and insufficient funds besides. I would be remiss to concede to your demands." He started tapping his pen again, looking out the window at the well-manicured gardens. "And, please, let's keep this civil. I don't want to have to bring security to escort you out."

Mom's face reddened. This was not good. For him. She leaned over the desk, her arms braced on the desk like two pillars supporting the face of some angry goddess. "Well, JP, it's not going to be civil. I'm a registered nurse. I recognize violations when I see them, and I see a whole bunch of them. From inadequate supervision to multiple health code violations. Serious cleanliness problems, JP. Serious. Now you listen and listen well: I want my father-in-law within an hour or I go to state authorities."

The man returned Mom's stare, paled, blinked his eyes a few times, and turned to his secretary.

"Marsha, fill out the necessary forms for Mr. Taylor to be discharged into the care of Ms. Taylor." A strained smile filled his face. "And if there is anything else we can do for you Ms. Taylor, please let us know."

Mom pushed off the desk, her eyes soft, the lioness replaced by a doe batting her eyelids.

"Yes," she replied sweetly, "one more thing."

A sigh escaped from Dr. J.P. Henry as though he had been holding his breath. His face had regained the slight smile which had been pasted on at the start of the conversation.

"Yes?"

"Address me as Mrs. Taylor right now, you arrogant son of a bitch."

His face flushed with anger, a vein in his necked throbbed. Dr. J.P. Henry looked out the window, weighing the consequences of his next words. Then he turned back to Mom.

"Yes, Mrs. Taylor," he spat out through clenched teeth.

She held his angry stare for a moment and walked out. I was so proud of her. Mom was like one of those well-built Mercedes: neat looking car on the outside, but rigid, inflexible iron on the inside.

At the time I didn't fully comprehend the ramifications of Mom's decision. We moved into Granddad's place that very day. Mom flew back to Florida while I took care of Gramps. Two weeks later she arrived at the cabin with our old van jammed with the clothes, books, electronics, and a few albums. Apparently it was going to be a long, long visit.

*

So, I came from Florida, where classes had already ended, to Western New York, where kids were preparing for some state tests called the Regents, from a city with seven major amusement parks and paintball galore to Redneckville, USA, where folks carry on about the sunset the night before and whether it's going to rain the next day, from a well-paying job for Mom at a nationally recognized hospital to a low paying one at a jumble of different buildings patched together and called Conaroga Hospital.

The golf courses in this area were not much more than cow pastures, not that it mattered to me anymore. I couldn't even afford the few dollars they asked for green fees. Nor could we afford cable TV. One of the local channels had a sportsman show in the evening which Gramps and I watched. Surfing the Internet wasn't an option either. We only had dial-up on a modem. All I could get was some news and a few sites without many pictures. Any music or videos required wait times from minutes to hours. Maybe we did the right thing in coming to Conaroga, but sometimes the right thing isn't the best thing, at least, not for me.

Mom took care of Gramps in the morning and afternoon; I watched him from the late afternoon until about midnight when she got back from her late shift.

Conaroga was a small village next to the Genesee River, a slow moving, mud filled stream that meandered all over the valley it had formed over the last million or so years. Summer for me in Conaroga flowed slower than the river. I made no friends. In part this was because I was pissed off about having to leave my home, but also because I was busy fixing things around the log cabin and taking care of Gramps. It made me kinda hate him. Yeah, I knew it wasn't fair, but I couldn't help it.

Actually, I did make one friend: Jerry. He saw me running one day. The next day I had a running mate, who slowed me down considerably. After our run... well, it wasn't much more than a fast walk... he showed me a path through the woods not far from his house. We emerged onto the edge of a high canyon wall, the brown ribbon of the Genesee River six hundred feet below. It was the first sight that impressed me in this backwater region, not as multi-dimensional or exciting as Disney World, or even Sea World, but still pretty cool.

He talked about his dad but never said much about his mom. The word divorce popped up in the middle of one sentence. It disappeared almost as though it never had been uttered. Obviously he didn't want to talk about it, so I didn't ask any questions. Anyway, both of us we're being raised in single parent homes. It really was our only connection. Jerry was a nice kid, but a bit of a dweeb and only an eighth-grader. And, my only friend. Hip-hip-hurray!

My new responsibilities would certainly rule out cross-country in the fall and track in the spring. Instead, I had to take care of Gramps. By the end of summer, I had pretty much resigned myself to a dreary year. After a few weeks at Conaroga Central, my expectations became a bitter reality. Today's encounter with Goatee man just added fear to my repertoire of complaints about Conaroga.

CHAPTER THREE

A minute after Mom left for work there was a knock. I left Gramps and hesitated at the door. Could it be the Goatee Man returning to confront Gramps? I opened the door a crack with my foot against the bottom. I was relieved to see only Mr. Songor, the neighbor across the road. A regular visitor, he strolled into the kitchen. "Hey Billy-boy, how are you doing today?"

He passed me to greet Gramps and I couldn't help but smile. He was one of the few friends who had not deserted Gramps when he got sick. Old friends from the early morning coffee clutch at Dunkin Donuts and his drinking buddies from Old Tavern never visited.

I met Mr. Songor in May when we first brought Gramps back to the cabin. He drove Granddad and me back and forth from stores in the village to the cabin. Actually, he wasn't one of those 'regular' friends; he had been Granddad's banker for many years. Mr. Songor's own father had Alzheimer's so he understood what we were going through.

A bit shorter than me, Mr. Songor had a bushy tuff of curly gray hair fighting a receding hairline. The few, but pronounced wrinkles in his face suggested he was old, but not as old as Gramps. Never ask me to peg down ages for anyone over thirty.

"Counting his fortune again?" Mr. Songor asked me with a wink.

"Well, separating quarters and nickels today."

"Could have used him in the bank years ago."

"Probably just as well he was on the other side of the counter, Mr. Songor."

His eyebrows pressed down and narrowed his eyes. "Hey, I told you to call me Kenny, young man."

"Kenny. Kenny. I'll try."

He pulled up a chair to sit down beside Gramps. Mr. Songor plucked a quarter from the small, but still mixed pile in the center of the table. "Want that over there, Pete?"

Gramps didn't look up, but he nodded his head, intent on the work. I left the two of them alone while I checked the dinner Mom had prepared and did some cleaning in the kitchen. Mr. Songor... Kenny... always seemed to be able to get Gramps to talk about the past. Gramps had plenty of stories to tell about Letchworth State Park where he had worked for over thirty years. The patient banker just listened, nodded, and sometimes asked questions even when it was the third or fourth time he might have heard a story.

Right now Granddad was mumbling about having tea with Albert Einstein somewhere in the park. I looked over to Mr. Songor and he winked at me.

"Sheppard's Pie for dinner, Mr. Son..." I stopped myself, "I mean, Kenny...wanna stay?"

He patted Gramps on the shoulder and got up. "Nope. Gotta get back to some spaghetti. The sauce is brewing right now." He kissed his finger like an Italian chef and threw his outstretched fingers out.

"It is, how you say, fantasamifico!" he announced in a fake Italian voice.

I walked him to the door.

"Strange thing happened to me on the way home today. When I was jogging home some guy nearly ran me over. Then he jumped out of car and kinda pushed me around. He said Gramps had better give him some money. Freaked me out."

Mr. Songor's face, which usually held a grin, now had uncharacteristic frown lines. "What did he look like, Billy?"

"About my height: pale, rail thin. But, the guy was strong, very strong. Oh, and he had a goatee."

Mr. Songor brought his hand to his chin and rubbed it as he stared at the ground. When he looked up, his furrowed brow resembled the look my father used to get when he was giving advice. My stomach clenched with the memory.

"Haven't seen anyone like him in town. Look, Billy...You'd best tell your mom."

"Yeah. I'll tell her for sure."

"Good. Now lock the door after I go. I doubt the guy is going to come back, but, you know, just in case. He comes back, call me first, then the police. I can get here quicker."

I gulped, but nodded. This was serious.

"Thanks, Mr. Songor."

The exaggerated scowl returned to his face.

"Kenny, I mean." I added, grinning and shaking my finger at him.

He winked, held his hand up and twisted some invisible lock in the air. I closed the door and locked it.

With Alzheimer's patients you have to keep routines. When Mom wasn't managing the schedule, I had to. Every night at 5:30 we had dinner. Tonight Gramps was trying to eat his food with his butter knife. I replaced it with his spoon and he quickly gobbled up the Sheppard's Pie and asked for more.

While I watched him eat, I realized I lost my father and had become a father, within a year. Memories of a robust, flamboyant, fun loving man fought their way back into my brain. My father, Gramps' son. A lump formed in my throat. I patted the old man gently on the back. It wasn't his fault he had Alzheimer's.

Halfway through the second helping, Gramps looked up at me. "Billy, it's not in Letchworth." Sometimes he's more lucid than others. I can tell because his eyes seem aimed right at mine. Then he says things, more clear than ever before, as though he wants to implant his last remaining memories in your brain so they won't be lost in the black pool of his disease. Sometimes, like this last one, the messages are cryptic.

"What do you mean Gramps?"

But, the moment was lost. The eyes were blank again. "Al and I at tea." He had slipped back to his silly stories.

"Yeah, Gramps - you and Albert Einstein."

His face reddened and he threw his spoon to the floor. "No! No! Al, tea, tea table. Al."

For some reason, he often gets agitated right before or during dinner. I tried to calm him down. "Okay, granddad, tea with Al."

Mollified, he looked around his plate for his spoon. I gave him mine and Gramps returned eating. I sighed, blowing out pent up air through my mouth. We were back to normal again, or what passed for normal. After he finished dinner, I let him play a bit more with the coins while I cleaned up the kitchen. When I picked it up his discarded spoon, I wondered why he got so agitated over me saying that Al was Albert Einstein.

I stood beside him for a minute and watched him meticulously separate the coins. "Let's get you ready for bed, okay?"

He nodded and I led him to the bathroom where I washed his face and helped him put on his pajamas. He walked into the bedroom we shared and slipped into bed. I pulled the covers over him and patted him on the shoulder. The frail old man who was once my boisterous grandfather instantly fell asleep.

I studied chemistry and math for an hour. After chemical symbols and complicated equations got tangled up in my brain, I decided it was time to zone out on some TV. I watched a Glee rerun and got a few good chuckles in before Gramps came out of the bedroom. He had been asleep for about two hours. He often got up in the middle of the night and just walked around opening cupboards as though he was looking for something. The doctor said it was normal and to just walk with him until he got tired. So, for an hour we walked all around the house together. He tried to go out the front door, but I distracted him with some ice cream. By the time he went back to bed, I was too tired to even watch TV. So, I washed my face and brushed my teeth and walked into the bedroom.

I stood over Gramps to make sure he was asleep. After these nocturnal strolls, he was usually a sound sleeper. Even my alarm clock in the morning didn't alter the rhythm of his snores.

I slipped into my own bed. The soft snoring annoyed me tonight. It was an irritating reminder about how much my life had changed. I put the pillow over my head. Before I finally drifted off to sleep, the snores were replaced with a sentence.

"Tea, Al. Tea."

When the snoring resumed, I drifted onto that calm black ocean called sleep. My last thought was a question, if not Einstein, then who was the Al in his story?

CHAPTER FOUR

My school in Florida had only sophomores, juniors, and seniors and there were over two thousand students in a modern complex bigger than most malls. Conaroga Central School was a single, two story ancient brick building that served less than one thousand students, kindergarten through twelfth grade. Walking toward the front door I watched little kids, holding hands or running past me while annoying squeals and screams from the junior high kids filled the air. The courtyard of the school was a kaleidoscope mix of students, some sporting designer jeans with neatly fitting jackets and some with Sponge Bob T-shirts. The visual and acoustical mayhem somehow organized itself just in time to enter the narrow front doors before the late bell. Jerry stuck by my side like one of those annoying burrs that stubbornly attached to your leg after a walk in tall grass.

"So, I played Guardian yesterday...got to level five." Jerry always interpreted my silence as an invitation to keep talking.

"It's pretty cool. Graphics aren't as good as Halo, but you got more ways to go. Have you played it yet?"

A question. I had to focus on his boring monologue. I replayed his ramblings in my brain and then answered. "You gotta go through the dungeon first. I got to level twelve that way."

He stopped and pulled on my jacket, twisting me around. In my peripheral vision, it seemed like a dozen heads swiveled towards us. I pried his hand away and kept walking, my face hot. In Florida I didn't even know any eighth-graders. Here, he's my only friend. Great. Just great.

I tried to convince myself I didn't care about what anyone thought, but, at the same time, I didn't want to be the weird new kid who hung out with an eighth-grader. I mean a junior with an eighth-grader was not the coolest thing even in Podunk territory. Jerry, however, didn't realize I was trying to ignore him. He looked up to me with a combination of admiration and excitement.

"You made it to level twelve? Oh, my gosh! You gotta show me how, Bill. Come over this afternoon and we can play."

He was pulling on my jacket again. Not cool. Not cool at all. One eyebrow raised, I looked down at his hand. He took the hint and let go. We walked into the building until we reached a T in the hallway; Jerry would go to the junior high wing and I could retreat to the senior high wing.

"Can't. Gotta get home right after school. See ya."

Of course Jerry waved goodbye to me making our association all the more obvious. While I walked down the hall there were a few chuckles. Before I could turn around and glare I was face to face with Sarah Seeley.

Books propped in her arms, a slight tilt of her head, she scrutinized me.

"Hey, Billy."

Butterflies flew in my stomach and then out my mouth. I sputtered: "Hi… Sarah."

She walked with me to the junior lockers. I hazarded a sideways glance at her. Her blue eyes were focused on some posters for the pep rally. She looked back at me and I quickly looked over her head at the same poster, nodding approval. I silently prayed she didn't see me with Jerry.

"I saw you talking to Jerry," she began. So much for the power of prayer.

Her simple sentence was a punch in my gut. My insides flipped upside down. I stopped and fidgeted with a strap on my book bag.

"Ahh… Jerry Smith. Oh yeah. Him. He… ahh… rides the same bus."

She started to say something but Rick Henson, star quarterback, grabbed her arm and leaned down to talk to her. For once I was grateful the egotistical jerk showed up. I was off the hot seat and spared from any comments about my junior high friend.

Rick easily pulled her away. They were girlfriend and boyfriend. She smiled over her shoulder at me and I nodded.

Sarah was in most of my classes and was my lab partner in chemistry. Once when she leaned into me during chemistry lab, her blond hair brushed across my face. It was soft with a faint aroma of peaches, her shampoo I supposed.

It wasn't difficult to stare at Sarah. She was just… I don't know… pretty. All the time. But when she smiled… well, then she was beautiful. I know it sounds stupid, but when she smiled I'd swear the room got brighter. And when she laughed, oh my God… it was just off the scales.

Yeah, I was smitten with her. No doubt about that. Not that any of my feelings mattered. Since she was tied to Rick Henson, my chances of connecting with her were essentially zero. And now she had seen me with my only friend, Jerry... an eighth-grader. I shook my head and sighed.

I got to homeroom, my face hot and breathing like I did at the end of a race. I clenched my jaw tight.and waited for the jokes and snide comments. All I got was a few disinterested glances and even fewer hellos. Sometimes being ignored isn't a bad thing.

The day went molasses-slow until seventh period when I had chemistry lab - with Sarah. Besides being really pretty, she was also nice. Really nice. Natural nice. So, I guess I could consider her friend. In school only. Hmm... she's not my girlfriend, but my school-friend. Okay. I can live with that. I guess.

I got to chemistry before my 'school-friend' arrived and watched Mr. Sneal, the science teacher, draw diagrams on the white board. Sarah strolled in, plopped her books down and sat right beside me. I took in a great breath and smelled that faint peach aroma again.

She reached into her book bag to get her notebook. I noted how the strands of her hair framed her ear. She looked up, noticed me watching her, and smiled. Flustered, I quickly diverted my eyes and clenched my fist so hard I almost cut the skin. I had to be more careful about staring at her. She would start to think I'm a perv or something.

After opening up her lab book, she finally turned to me with a half-smile. "Hi, Billy."

I realized then I was as mute as a statue, not giving any greeting. My mouth was so dry, my tongue stuck to the top of my mouth and I grunted "Hey Salah." Oh, God. Can I be any more of a klutz? I waited for the quip about Jerry. I could feel my face adopt the same grimness a condemned criminal must have when he faces the electric chair. Spare me the agony of waiting for it, Sarah. Pull the switch quickly, please.

The loud "smack" startled me and I jumped. Sarah giggled. I shouldn't have reacted that way. Mr. Sneal started all his classes by banging the meter stick on the demonstration table.

Mr. Sneal's nasally voice began the lab. "All right. This lab is on titration…"

A few minutes later I was adjusting the glass knob and controlling the flow of weak acid into the beaker filled with water and some chemical, phenol-something. Sarah watched intently and then tried it herself. When the clear solution turned purple she grinned and I couldn't help but smile at her reaction and the chemical one. Mr. Sneal often stressed how chemistry changed our lives. In a way, different from what Mr. Sneal had probably intended, chemistry had certainly changed mine.

As the lab progressed I became more relaxed. Apparently Sarah wasn't going to rib me about being with Jerry. The 'dream' stubbornly resurrected itself. Maybe, just maybe, I might have a chance with her. I even joked with her and was rewarded with a few laughs. The dull yellow paint in the chemistry room transmuted to a brilliant gold.

As we cleaned up our table, she stopped momentarily and gently bit her lower lip as she looked down at the table. After I brought the clean test tube back, she caught my eye.

"Bill, I saw you talking to Jerry Smith this morning."

No butterflies now. Just a fifty pound metal weight pulling my stomach down. My jaw clenched tight again. It was starting to hurt. I stared at the last test tube lying on the lab bench. I should pick it up, but I was paralyzed and waited for ridicule.

"I just wanted you to know I think that was really nice of you to spend time with Jerry. I know he's gone through some rough times. I used to be his babysitter."

I looked up at her, my eyes wide with disbelief. She seemed to be pondering me as though she was looking at some picture in a museum. Her head was tilted, her eyes were scrunched together, and she held a finger to her lips. Very cute, of course, but a bit disconcerting as well.

"Yup. You're a nice guy, Bill Taylor," she said, nodding slightly up and down.

I managed to mumble something. I don't know what I said and it's probably just as well I've forgotten. My face was hot again, and I fumbled with the test tube, almost breaking it.

"Hey, careful. You could cut yourself, Billy."

I looked up, quip on my tongue, smile on my face until I saw the long face of Rick Henson kissing Sarah's neck. She giggled, her head pressed down toward her shoulder trying squeeze him away. His arm went around her shoulder and he looked down at me. It was a cold day but he was wearing a designer T-shirt showing off a sculptured chest and long, muscular arms.

"Hey, Bill, who was your little friend you came in with this morning? New classmate?"

Before I could respond, Sarah pushed him away.

"You know who that was, Rick! Don't be such a jerk." She glared at Rick. Pretty from my vantage point, but I don't think Henson appreciated her natural beauty right now.

He put his hands up as though he was defending himself. "Hey, just wondering who his friends are."

Hands on hips, Sarah leaned into to him. "Well, me for one. Actually Billy and I are going to hang out this afternoon working on a chemistry lab."

The smug smile fell from Rick's face.

"Oh, well, cool. Yeah. He can do that." Then he looked at me, his eyes like daggers. "Just don't forget whose girl she is, right?"

I didn't say anything. Not because I was trying to be cool (I don't know how to be cool at all. Trust me on this). Not because

I didn't agree with him. He was right, of course. Definitely his girl. No, I didn't say anything because I was wondering if she really did plan to have me help her. I had to watch Gramps. I started to speak to her and explain my predicament when Rick, his arm now locked around her shoulders, walked her out of the class.

CHAPTER FIVE

Right after classes I found Sarah waiting for me at my locker. She was biting that lower lip again.

"About the lab stuff... getting together so you can help me... I'm sorry. I don't know why I said it."

Disappointed and relieved at the same time, I didn't know what to say. Actually, I didn't have to say anything at all because she quickly continued, nearly yelling.

"Yes, I do. Rick can be such a jerk at times. Ever since he made All-County quarterback last year when he was just a sophomore."

Great. All-County quarterback as a sophomore. Just a few bragging points there.

"Then when he was selected for the National Honor Society..." Sarah shook her head slowly and looked away from me for a moment, thinking.

"Uh-huh." Was all I could get out. National Honor Society too. Not bad, Rick.

"He's just so full of himself, it's like...I don't know; he acts like you should thank him for the honor of being close to him."

She looked away for a moment. I thought I saw tears welling in her eyes, but her jaw was clenched like she was pissed.

"Anyway, I just didn't want him to think he could be mean to you. I was going to ask you for some help anyway..." Then her voice dropped off.

I hesitated. She looked down the empty hallway.

"I understand. It was stupid, anyway."

Finally I found my voice...

"No, no, Sarah. I don't mind helping you. I would like to. But I can't. I... I just gotta go home."

The hallway brightened when she turned back to me, a great smile on her face.

"No problem, we could do it at your place. I'll get my books."

She zipped around the corner and I trotted after her telling her I rode the bus.

Sarah smiled over her shoulder. "Don't worry, we can take my car."

Oh, great. Just perfect. She has a car and I have to run two miles to the house when I get off a dilapidated school bus.

On our way to the student parking lot, I stepped into Bus 22. Old Tom, with a great grin on his face, was pondering the gas gauge.

"Gas day today," he announced. I never knew a guy who enjoyed filling up his gas tank as much as Tom. He always made a point of telling me and anyone else who would listen.

"Tom, just wanted to tell you I'm getting a ride home."

Tom leaned on the steering wheel to look behind me and saw Sarah.

When he looked back at me he chuckled. "You gonna have her drop you off at the bottom of the hill?"

I smiled, stepping off the bus. "Think I'll forego the run today."

Sarah's 'car' was actually a brand new Mustang. She got it from her lawyer "daddy" for her sixteenth birthday. Okay, she's

34

rich, I'm poor. I took a deep breath as we pulled out of the school parking lot.

"Sarah, I gotta tell you a few things." I hesitated a moment and then said very quickly, "I have to go home to take care of my grandfather. He's got Alzheimer's."

She turned to me, a frown on her face and then back to the road. Well, my stupid situation at home drove the last nail into the coffin.

"You don't have a nurse looking after him?"

Oh, boy. She wasn't making this easy, was she? I took a deep breath and blew out my mouth. Better to pull the band aid off fast. "No, we can't afford a nurse. We live in his house... well, it's a cabin... and take care of him. My mom and me. She watches him during the day then goes to work at the hospital. I watch him at night. At least till midnight when she gets back."

Sarah was quiet for a few seconds, probably regretting knowing me, let alone getting help from me.

"My grandma has Alzheimer's too. She's in a nursing home."

"So was Gramps. But we took him out. It... ahh... it wasn't a good nursing home."

She looked at me again. A new look. Not pity, maybe concern, or maybe she was trying to figure out how to dump me before we got to the cabin.

"How far along is he? I mean he can talk and stuff, can't he?"

"Oh, yeah. He gets confused sometimes. And he loves to count money. Well, he thinks he's counting dollars. He separates nickels and dimes by size and says thing like 'dollar here' and 'dollar' there."

She giggled, quick like she was relieved and then spoke more seriously. "Well, at least he keeps busy. My grandma just stares at the floor and just picks at the table cloth. It kinda hurts seeing her like that."

We pulled into the driveway and walked in the house. Mom, her back to us, was in the kitchen finishing the dishes from lunch.

"Mom, I brought a friend home to study some chemistry."

My mother wiped her hands, turned, a grand smile on her face for the first friend I brought into the cabin, and saw Sarah. Her smile faded. She had this rule about me having a girl in the house when she wasn't home. Simple rule. Never.

Sarah walked up to her, grinning. A golfer with a nine iron raised high, running up a hill in a thunderstorm, had a better chance of survival. "Hi, Mrs. Taylor. I'm Sarah Seeley. Bill has been helping me with chemistry. I hope it's all right if I get some more help this afternoon."

Mom weakly returned the smile and shook her hand. Sarah looked at granddad hunched over the table separating coins. Over her head, Mom glared at me. I got the 'why didn't you tell me' look. All I could do was raise my eyebrows, grimace, and shrug. Then she looked back at Sarah and sighed. How could anyone not like Sarah?

"No, it's fine. Stay for dinner if you'd like. Just make sure you call your folks to let them know you're here. I have to run now, kids. Late for my shift at the hospital. Sarah, nice to meet you, dear."

Wow. I know now how it feels to have an execution commuted to life in prison. A kiss for me... super, no embarrassment there... and Mom was gone. I motioned Sarah to the living room. Granddad had his old Buffalo Bills hat on, slightly askew and was separating the coins again.

"Hi Gramps. This is Sarah." I neaten the cap on his head.

The tired eyes looked up at Sarah and a grin lit his face.

"Oh, Johnny, you brought Abby back."

He grabbed both our hands as though he was performing some ceremony. Sarah looked at me with a half-smile, her forehead wrinkled in confusion.

"Yeah, brought her back, Pop."

"Good. Good. Like you in my home."

Sarah grinned back at him.

"You especially, Abby." He said with a wink. "Johnny you should bring her by more often. Stay for dinner, Abby?"

"Why, I'd love to, Mr. Taylor! If it's OK with... Johnny" she smiled at me, her eyes twinkling.

'Johnny' didn't have a chance to say yea or nay as granddad brought her hand to his cheek and held it there a moment. Then he went back to his coins and we didn't exist for him anymore.

It was settled. Sarah would stay for dinner. We returned to the kitchen.

"He's adorable" she smiled as she looked back at Gramps. "So, I'm Abby and you're Johnny?"

"Abby is my mom's name. And Johnny was my dad's name."

"I know your mom works at the hospital, where does your dad work?"

I watched the old man separating coins by the warm wood stove.

"He... ahh... he died of cancer. Last year."

Her hand went toward mine, but she pulled back. "Oh, Billy. I'm so sorry."

I couldn't help it... tears formed in my eyes. I turned away from her toward the counter. It was clean, but I wiped it down. Coughed to clear my throat, my back to her.

Sarah touched my shoulder.

"Tell me about him."

I shook my head and stirred the stew.

"He... ahh... he was a really great guy. Loud and laughing. Dad was a hugger...God I used to get so embarrassed at how much he'd hug me." I chuckled but a sob broke it and I took a great breath of air. I closed my eyes. How much I would give to have one more hug now. A few tears fell to the floor, but she didn't see them. At least I hoped she didn't. I coughed again.

"He would take me rock climbing, jog with me, play cards. No matter what we did, it was fun to be with him."

Sarah said nothing. The silence was embarrassing so I just kept talking.

"When the cancer came, we all fought it. Him most of all. But some things you can't beat. He couldn't beat cancer. Anyway, Gramps sometimes thinks I'm him."

I went to the bathroom and washed my face. When I returned she was looking at some pictures plastered over the fridge.

"Who are these guys?" she asked. Sarah pointed to a picture of myself and two of my friends holding up a girl in a bikini above blue ocean water.

"Guy in the center was Jim. It was his girlfriend we were holding. He was a year ahead of me, but we all hung out together. Joe's holding her feet, he's my best friend."

For a moment, I stared at my own image, almost unrecognizable. I was shorter then but just as lean. Brown eyes, a pronounced jawline which I thought made me good looking. A straight nose, maybe a bit too large. Now I lacked the tan and the long hair. And, the smile.

I read somewhere that the Mayans in Mexico fashioned rubber balls, rubber bands, and rubber soles three thousand years ago. Rubber, three thousand years ago! Unbelievable. After their civilization collapsed with the arrival of the Cortez and the other Spanish, the technique was forgotten by all but a few isolated tribes. Our departure from Florida was my Cortez. I had pretty much forgotten how to smile anymore. When I looked at myself in a mirror these days, it seemed like my face was beginning to harden into a perpetual frown.

"You look happy in that picture."

"Yeah. I was happy then."

She looked at me strangely for a moment, turned and went to the table to take out her lab book.

The next half hour found me explaining how to frame her report, to be concise but including all the important stuff. In the end her report was short and clear. Then I quickly constructed mine, taking care to insure it was different from hers. I wouldn't want Sneal thinking she had copied mine.

"Thanks so much Billy. I actually get it now. You should be a teacher!"

"After Dad worked in the salt mine in Retsof, he became a teacher. History. Who knows? Maybe it's in my blood, huh?"

I plopped the stew in some bowls and put out some bread and butter while she talked with Gramps. Her laughter bounced into the kitchen and a grin cracked the frozen landscape of my face. Sarah led Gramps into the kitchen, praising and reassuring him at the same time. Gramps was all smiles.

With dinner, I had to help Gramps with his spoon. Sarah leaned over him and wiped away a bit of gravy on his face.

After dinner she helped me clean up, and we chatted about music and movies. When we were done, it was dark out.

"I'd better get home." She kissed Gramps on the cheek and said goodbye. Boy, that got a big smile. Then she picked up her books. At the door, she hesitated.

"I really, really enjoyed the whole afternoon, Billy. And the dinner was great. Thanks." She looked over my shoulder and yelled goodbye to Gramps. His hand went up for a wave, but a moment later he was back counting coins. She looked at me, smiled, turned and walked to her car. As I watched her drive away I realized I had been smiling for most of the evening.

If I had a crystal ball showing me the days ahead, I wouldn't have been smiling at all.

CHAPTER SIX

The next morning, I bounded into the kitchen whistling. Mom stirred oatmeal into some boiling milk.

"So, how did it go with Sarah?"

"It was all right. I mean, you know. We studied chemistry and stuff." I started pushing the lever on the toaster up and down. Then I studied the toaster as though it wasn't working right. Mom wasn't fooled by my absurd behavior.

"And 'stuff'?" she asked, stirring the hot cereal.

"Gramps, dinner. She liked dinner."

"So, a good time?"

She was looking at me strangely as I turned the toaster over, crumbs falling on the counter. "Hmm." I said, pretending to inspect the bottom of the toaster. Then I returned the toaster to its perch and wiped down the counter. "Yeah. Well, it's okay. Nothing special. You know, just friends."

Mom took the oatmeal off the stove and filled my bowl. Gramps was still sleeping. Sprinkled with cinnamon and sweetened with real maple syrup (the one luxury Mom insisted on continuing), I covered it with cold milk and shoveled three spoonsful in my mouth. Ha! Couldn't talk now. Before I could fill my mouth up again, Mom sat down and continued the

41

conversation. "I'm happy you're finally making some friends. Why don't you ask her out this weekend?"

She looked at the schedule on the refrigerator and continued, "I can take care of things around here." By 'things around here' she meant Gramps.

"Nah. We're just friends."

"Well, friends can just go out. Besides, I'm pretty sure she likes you, Billy."

"Mom, she already has a boyfriend."

"Hmm… "

Whenever Mom says 'Hmm' she wants to say something but doesn't. Like the time Dad took me rock-climbing in Tennessee. Mom said "Hmm… " and later I heard them arguing. Dad still took me though.

I didn't go for the bait and ask her what she meant by 'Hmm.' In fact, I decided it was a good time to change the subject.

"Mom, yesterday some weird guy stopped me on the way home. He said something about Gramps giving him some money. Like a threat."

"He just talked to you?"

"Yeah. Well, he pushed me too."

Mom's smiles from our earlier conversation disappeared. She had the same look on her face when she rescued Gramps from the nursing home.

Jaws clenched, her face frozen, she reached for the phone.

Alarmed, I asked, "What are you doing?"

She didn't answer. At least not with words. I got the 'look.' The 'look' trumped everything else. It made 'Hmm' ho hum. You don't dare say or ask anything when you got the 'look.'

"I want to talk to the police chief," Mom said into the phone.

Unfortunately, whoever was on the other end, didn't see the 'look', but they quickly got the verbal equivalent.

An Officer Smith was at our door within ten minutes. This, at least, was better than Florida. There we reported a robbery last year, and the cops didn't come around until three days later.

Officer Smith had short curly black hair peppered with gray. We sat down at the kitchen table and he asked me a dozen questions, writing notes down on a pad. All the while, Mom sat with her arms folded, monitoring the investigation. Half an hour later, we sat in silence as he flipped through the pages, reviewing everything. He met Mom's cold stare head on, a feat not many dared and even fewer survived.

"We'll be on the lookout for the car, Mrs. Taylor. The chief will have patrol cars drive past your house for a while. If we see this guy, we'll talk to him. Should discourage him. If anything else happens call us. Look, I live down at the end of the road. Here's my home number. Feel free to call me if you have any concerns at all." I looked at his name tag again and it finally clicked.

"Wait, Officer Smith. You must be Jerry's dad."

"Yeah. I figured you must be the Bill he's been talking about. He thinks the world of you, young man. It's Bill this or Bill that. Hey, I know he can talk the ears off of corn stalks. Thanks for being so patient."

I was uneasy with the compliment since my thoughts were not always as nice as my words.

Officer Smith left and Mom got Gramps up. We dressed him and plopped him in the car. She dropped me off at school. I missed English and gym, but that was all right. Chemistry (without the lab) was fourth period. When I got to chemistry, I quickly looked for Sarah. Stupid, but I couldn't stop myself. With a few books held in front of her, she was swaying back and forth behind Rick who was talking to a few of his football buddies.

She looked bored. When she saw me, she waved and strolled over to greet me.

"Hey Billy! Thanks again for your help last night. I think I could use a study session for the test next week. You up for it?"

"Oh, yeah, sure. Fine. No, I can help again. Glad to. Really, I am. Yup. I can help."

After the words tumbled out, I wanted to crawl in a hole. A simple 'sure' was all that was required. But, no, I had diarrhea mouth. God, why am I such an idiot around her?

"Well, next week before Friday then…"

"Yes, next week. Monday. Wednesday. Thursday even. Sure. Yes, that's great. You drive. I mean, if it's all right, you can drive me home. I could walk. I mean run, take the bus…"

Sarah gave me a quizzical look and a half smile. "Good, Wednesday, I'll let you know when I get done with cheerleading practice." She stared at me for a moment and left to sit down. I know what the stare was about. She was having second thoughts about spending too much time with flapper-jaw.

After class, Sarah left with Rick. When they passed my chair, she winked and smiled at me. With Rick looking over her head, I just nodded, suppressing a big smile.

I walked alone down the hall to Spanish. There were some nice drawings posted on the walls. I noticed how the building was much cleaner than my school in Florida. I nodded at a few of the students I recognized from my classes. They smiled and a few even greeted me by name. Maybe Conaroga wouldn't be so bad after all.

After Spanish I walked alone to the cafeteria for lunch. Rick Henson and a few of his jock friends were clustered together in the hallway right outside the cafeteria door. One of the larger guys, a tackle on the football team, pointed to me. Rick's head swiveled and he stepped away from the group. His eyes on me,

44

he nudged his head toward the cluster. "Hey, Taylor. Come 'ere. Settle a debate for us, Chem Whiz." I didn't like to be ordered around, but I didn't want to appear scared or stuck up either. So, I stopped in front of the group. Rick tossed his thumb toward the big tackle.

"Jim here claims that different people have different athletic skills. Like a guy might be good in football, but suck at baseball. I'm thinking good athletes can do well in any sport. If you're great at football, you'd be great at baseball, track, heck, even bowling. What do you think?"

I considered the question with my brows knitted together. Was this some kind of test or initiation rite? Something was up with these guys so I answered cautiously. "I don't know. I guess good athletes would be okay with any sport, but they might excel in only a few."

Rick nodded thoughtfully, looking at his friends who were snickering. A few more of the juniors stood around us listening. I saw Sarah wedge her way in through the growing crowd.

"Well, it looks like you and I have a disagreement then. I think a really good athlete is naturally good at every other sport," Rick continued. Then he smacked his head and opened his eyes wide.

"Geez. What an opportunity! We could have an experiment, Taylor. You do well with experiments, don't you? I mean you helped Sarah do them and all." A few chuckles followed his observation.

I tilted my head and scrunched my face. What was going on here?

"No, no... this will be cool. Trust me," he said. I'm thinking a used car salesman selling a freshly painted 2003 Trans Am would be safer to trust.

"Look, you're a runner and I hear you're pretty good. I throw footballs. I'm pretty good at that." Nods all around confirming his last statement.

"Two entirely different sports," he continued. "Two entirely different guys. But, I'm saying that a good athlete will be just as good in any sport. So, how about a race between you and me? If you're right, you should beat me. If I'm right, I'll beat you. An experiment to decide the debate, Chem Whiz. Whatta ya say?"

I didn't know where this was going. I looked over to Sarah who rolled her eyes.

"I guess. But, we're in school now, Rick."

"Hey, no problem. The track is just outside the cafeteria door. Let's go have a race before lunch."

Yeah, it was set up, all right. But, backing down wasn't an option.

"Okay. I guess."

He patted me on the back, a bit too hard to be friendly. "Great. Great. What kind of race? How about the 100 meter dash?"

Then I saw the trap. In the scrimmages this year, Rick scored nearly as many touchdowns running as he did passing. The guy was incredibly fast. His legs were longer than mine and he was at least just as quick. He'd beat me in a short race.

I looked out at the track through the windows. "How about four times around the track?"

He balked at that. He followed my stare, tilted his head and gritted his teeth. Then he turned back to me, his face scrunched up like he just ate a lemon. If I could get him to compete in a long race, I could beat him. Either he would have to back down or give me the advantage. I decided to push him just a bit.

46

"I mean, if you are a great athlete, Rick, you should be able to outrun me even on a long race. Isn't that what your theory suggests?"

He nodded. I had him. Just a little nudge now. "So, whadda ya say, Football Star?"

He glared at me.

"All right. You got it, Taylor. I'll do it!"

Within seconds the noise in the cafeteria heightened with news of the race. Chairs screeched. There were cheers as we headed out into the sunshine of the afternoon. Nearly one hundred kids and two or three nervous lunch monitors had followed us to watch the race. Rick was surrounded by his cronies who patted him on the back and laughed when they looked at me.

While I was stretching my legs, Jerry and a few of his eighth grade buddies surrounded me.

"You can do it, Bill. You can beat him. We know you can!"

"Thanks, little buddy. I think I can beat him, too."

I heard a voice behind me.

"You idiot."

I turned around to see Sarah.

"Sarah, you don't understand. Long distance runs are what I do best. I run two miles every day."

She shook that pretty little head of hers. Was she angry at me or scared for me?

"Rick set you up so well, Billy. He's run track for three years in a row. He was the sectional champ in the mile last year... as a sophomore."

I stared at her with my eyes opened as wide as my mouth.

"He just wants a chance to show you up. And you gave it to him on a platter with all the trimmings."

47

She then went to join some of her friends on the edge of the track. Rick had taken off his button down shirt and once again I faced those rock-hard muscles. There was not an ounce of fat on his body. His long legs looked like they would come up to my stomach. Smart move, Taylor. Smart, smart move.

There were no starting blocks. So we agreed to start from a crouched position. Everyone was quiet while Jim counted off "One... two... three... Go!"

He sprinted off, establishing a twenty yard lead. I was sorely tempted to keep up with him, but I restrained myself and kept my own pace. He took an even more commanding lead as we made the first turn. Those long legs kept putting greater and greater distance between us. When we reached the cheering crowd at the end of the first loop, I was thirty yards behind.

On the second loop, I maintained my long distance pace and I was forty yards behind.

On the third loop I increased my pace just a bit so by the time we reached the roaring crowd I was only twenty yards behind. If Rick started sprinting before me, I probably would not be able to make up the distance. Flushed and sweating, he was straining. Nevertheless, getting him to slow down was not going to happen.

I stayed the same distance behind him. He always looked over his right shoulder every five or so seconds to check my progress. I had swung out a bit to the right so he could more easily see me. My hope was that he was thinking he could out sprint me with a final burst of energy when he saw me starting my sprint. Tired as he was, Rick was reluctant to start his sprint too early.

At the halfway point of the final lap, he once again noted I was in the same position. I made my move. I started my sprint on his left side just as he looked away. In the subsequent five seconds I pulled within five yards of him. He looked over his shoulder once and then twice. That cost him a step or two. The next time he saw me, I had pulled up ahead of him on his left hand side.

Now we were both sprinting to the finish line. I was winded, but my breathing was steady, not like the heaving, deep breathing I heard behind me. As we came to the finish line, I willed my legs to move even quicker and somehow maintained my five yard advantage. At the finish line all I heard was his gasp of fatigue and everyone else's gasp of surprise.

I jogged a couple dozen steps and gradually slowed down. Rick veered to the right and caught his breath, hands on hips, head and torso parallel to the ground. I hoped he was going to vomit, but he didn't.

I walked back to shake his hand which he allowed but quickly let go. Between gasps he said, "You tricked me."

"I just ran my race, Rick."

By then we were surrounded by some of his friends. Most had gone inside for lunch. Rick and his crew left to go into the cafeteria. I heard Rick telling others I had tricked him. In a moment, I was alone. Well, nearly alone. Jerry Smith and some other eighth-graders came over.

"I knew you could do it, Bill. You beat him good."

"He's a good runner, Jerry. I was mostly lucky."

Sarah was waiting by the door. Jerry took the hint and waved to his friends to follow him to get their lunch.

"You keep surprising me, Bill Taylor."

I laughed. "Sometimes I surprise myself."

We walked into the cafeteria together and then went our separate ways, she to the junior tables and me to the corner again, joined by Jerry and few of his friends.

Yes, I had won the race. Unfortunately, not much changed. Except that I gained an enemy. Rick glared at me during the entire lunch period. My world was becoming more and more complicated. Just how complicated, I found out the next morning.

CHAPTER SEVEN

I was eating Cheerios when the local news announced a murder in Rochester. I looked up between bites and almost choked. The picture of the deceased on the screen looked like Mr. Goatee but without the goatee.

"Jeb Muzurki was found dead in his home on Clinton Avenue."

A video appeared with police cars parked in front of a small two story house.

"The authorities have no suspects. However, his connection with the 1992 Brink's Robbery heist suggests mafia ties."

Her back to me, Mom was putting away some dishes. "Wow! In Rochester. Murder and the mafia. And I thought we moved away from all that."

"Mom, I think that was the guy," I said slowly.

She turned around, her eyebrow slightly raised. "The guy who stopped you?"

Watching the newscast, my head went up and down.

"Are you sure?"

"Yeah, I'm pretty sure it's the same guy."

"We have to tell the police." Three hours later, Mom and I were sitting at the kitchen table talking with two detectives from

Rochester, one silver-haired and the other much younger. Mr. Smith, in uniform, monitored the proceedings as he stood by the refrigerator.

The older detective pointed to a glossy picture taken out of a folder. It showed a man, arms folded, leaning back against an old green car. A thin man with a goatee. "You're sure this is the guy who accosted you three days ago."

"Yes, sir. I'm sure about him and that's the car he was driving." I answered.

"And he said something about getting his share of the money?"

"He said he wanted his 'cut.'"

The two men looked at each other. The silver haired detective connected with my eyes.

"Billy, Jeb Muzurki was involved in a Brinks' robbery twenty years ago. Half the money is missing. Gone. Disappeared. Even the mafia doesn't know what happened to it."

"How much money?" asked Mom.

He turned to her and said, "Three million dollars."

The detective looked down at his notes and then back at Mom.

"Apparently, Jeb thought that your father-in-law knows something about the case."

He paused a moment and looked over at Gramps.

"Mrs. Taylor, can we talk to your father-in-law?"

Mom blinked a few times. Her voice was steady and firm.

"No. He's got Alzheimer's. You won't get anything out of him and, besides, I don't want to stress him."

"Ma'am, just a few questions, he might know something about the missing money. You can stop us anytime you want."

While she stared at Gramps, a clenched fist went to her lips. She looked back at the detective. "No. I don't feel good about doing that."

"It's important, ma'am," the silver-haired detective pleaded.

Mom gritted her teeth and shook her head. The other detective, hawk-nosed and sour-faced, leaned forward.

"Look. This is important…"

Officer Smith took two steps and was beside her.

"Mrs. Taylor has made it perfectly clear she does not want that to happen. Let's drop it."

Hawk-nose glared at Officer Smith and he looked back at him with this flat stare. When the young detective took a step closer to Officer Smith and stood nose to nose with him, his older partner spoke up.

"We understand, Mrs. Taylor. Here's my card. Call me if Billy recalls anything else." He rose and pulled Hawk-nose away. They walked toward the front door, followed by Mr. Smith. Then the older detective turned and added: "Or if some other incident happens."

"What do you mean 'some other incident'?" Mom asked nervously.

The detective stopped at the front door and turned around. "Mrs. Taylor, three men were incarcerated over this robbery. All served twenty years. All have just been released."

"You think they might come here?"

"Don't know ma'am since I don't know what your father-in-law knows."

She looked at the card and nodded. The two detectives left. Mom turned to Officer Smith, who waited at the door.

"Ben, thanks for your help."

"That's why the chief wanted me here during the interview. These Rochester detectives can be pushy at times."

"Do you think they can force Pete talk to them?"

He thought a moment. "I don't know. But, you may want to talk to a lawyer."

Mom nodded and said goodbye to him. When she returned to the kitchen, she was frowning. She looked at Gramps and then out the window. She breathed loudly, kinda hyperventilated. I saw her like this a couple of times as she got phone calls from the hospital about Dad.

"Mom, what's the big deal? Gramps won't know anything."

She ran her hands through her hair. Her face used to be perfectly smooth from any lines except smile lines, but dad's death and subsequent worries about our finances had added too many frown lines. She looked out the window as though the answer to my question was out there.

She took a deep breath and returned to normal breathing. "Your dad told me that Gramps had a problem with gambling years ago. A serious one. He owed thousands of dollars to some guys in Rochester. Gangsters."

My eyes widened to the size of quarters. I looked at the hunched figure at the table. Gramps? A gambler? Owing thousands of dollars?

"He paid it off somehow and then stopped gambling. All this happened before I met your Dad. It might have been in the early nineties. Billy, if he was involved it would explain how he paid off the debt."

We watched Gramps. His baseball cap slightly askew, he was mumbling 'dollar here' and 'dollar there.' I shook my head like a dog shaking off water, but I was shaking off the bits and pieces of unbelievable possibilities. This was the same man who proudly showed me commendations for his service as a park ranger. The same man who held my hand in the woods while he showed me bear tracks or pointed out and named a butterfly. I looked at my mother.

"Mom, come on. Granddad? He was a park ranger."

She looked away from Gramps to me.

"Maybe you're right," she conceded. "But let's take Ben's advice and talk with a lawyer, just in case."

When legal matters were involved Mom didn't cut corners. The lawyer with the biggest ad in the yellow pages was Henry Seeley. Sarah's dad. Mom dialed his number.

CHAPTER EIGHT

We managed to get an appointment with Mr. Seeley just after lunch. Mr. Songor watched Gramps while we were gone. Seeley's office was located in a professional building on the edge of the village. We sat in plush chairs in the waiting room, and a well-dressed, middle-aged secretary asked us if we wanted something to drink.

"Espresso, Perrier's, a Coke for you, young man?" We declined and she went back to her work, smiling up at us every so often. Mom was fidgeting the same way she did when we waited for the hospital accountant after Dad died. When riled, her face was fierce and few could handle the stare and even fewer dared to respond to her words that could be razor-edged sharp. But, when faced with personal problems, she was like a nail-biting kid waiting for punishment. She was biting her nails now. The outer door opened and a tall, older man swept through the waiting room, not even giving us a nod. Attorney Seeley.

A minute later, a younger man with a tie, loosely knotted, and rolled up sleeves, stuck his head outside a door and waved us into his office. He took down some information, put it in a folder, and asked for payment. Two hundred dollars for the consultation. Two hundred dollars! Mom glared at the assistant.

She threw her one credit card across the desk as though she didn't want to dirty her hands with the transaction.

Then the same young man escorted us into Mr. Seeley's office. When I sat down in a leather chair I saw on the large mahogany desk a picture of Sarah and an attractive older woman, undoubtedly Sarah's mom. Mr. Seeley came in, acknowledged us warmly, presumably because we're now paying customers, and sat down behind his desk. After about fifteen minutes of talking we had what we came for.

"So, they can't force him to talk?" Mom asked, her face twisted with concern.

"Not if he has brain impairment specified by a doctor. Advanced Alzheimer's falls under that category, Mrs. Taylor. And, even if you let him talk, any statements are inadmissible in a court of law."

"If they show up at the house..."

"You are within your rights to deny them access to Mr. Taylor. They can't meet with him without your consent."

She thanked Mr. Seeley and we left. In the van Mom's face was clenched tight and her hands were white on the steering wheel.

"No detectives?" I asked.

"Absolutely not! There's nothing he can tell them anyway, even if he was part of that robbery."

After dinner, the phone rang. Mom picked it up and smiled. She looked at me while she chatted. Mom didn't get many calls so I was curious. After a moment or so she handed me the phone. It was Sarah. She was worried about me when I didn't show up for school. I told her about the murder, the detectives, and that we went to see her Dad. "He's good." He should be, I thought to myself. On the way home I had calculated that he made the equivalent of eight-hundred dollars an hour for our consultation. That's about what Mom makes in two weeks. I said nothing about Gramp's gambling problem.

Sarah filled me in on some things I missed at school.

After I hung up, Mom looked at me and said, "Friends, huh?"

I rolled my eyes and went to my room to catch up on the assignments.

The next day in study hall, I checked out to the library explaining I had a history paper to research. I did have a term paper coming up after Christmas and I should have been doing research on it. Instead, I went to Wikipedia to find out about a robbery twenty years before. I had just started reading the article when someone covered my eyes with soft, small hands.

"Guess who?"

"Ahh... Tammy?"

Sarah laughed, sat next to me, and nudged me playfully.

"Watcha doing?"

"Doing research for history. About a robbery."

"A robbery?"

"Yeah, well, a Brinks' armored car robbery. Kinda of a mystery."

I pointed to a line on the screen.

"In Henrietta. Right outside a Dunkin' Donuts."

She bumped me with her shoulder. "Get out!"

The librarian, an ancient creature with snow white hair, cleared her throat and glared at us over her glasses. The library had always been a quiet place to study, for decades apparently.

"No, read right here." I whispered.

Sarah pressed against my shoulder looking at the page. I didn't scoot away.

"Cool, maybe the missing money was buried somewhere around here." Sarah said excitedly. The librarian cleared her throat again.

"Buried money? Why did you say that?" I whispered, pretending to look at the screen.

She thought a moment and then answered so quietly that my head inclined closer to her. "I don't know. A robbery, missing money. A buried treasure is cool, I guess."

I turned to her.

"Buried treasure?" I shook my head, confused. "Sarah, it was an armored car robbery."

Her brow furrowed (very cute).

"Oh, that's right, I forgot the rules. If it was an armored car robbery, then criminals aren't allowed to bury the money," she hissed.

"No. Yes. All right, maybe. But unlikely. It's more likely some criminal has the money and probably spent it all."

"Did it say that in the article?" Her voice might be audible to the next table (no one was there), but who knows what the white-haired crone forty feet away could detect. She was watching us, a hawk fixed on running mice.

I shifted in my seat and coughed. At the end of the cough, I whispered, "Not so loud."

Sarah was quiet.

"The mafia was involved and the article implied that someone in the mafia might have taken the money," I whispered barely moving my lips.

"Then how do you know it isn't buried?"

My forehead wrinkled. She had twisted me around to concede her initial outlandish assumption. "I don't know. I mean it could be buried." But that was stupid, of course, and I wanted to scream it to her. Then I looked at up at the librarian, who, thankfully, was busy writing something down. Probably notes about our noisy behavior. I looked back to Sarah.

She had been scanning the page. Her finger pointed to a line on the screen.

"Billy," she whispered, "Six million dollars!"

"Two men jumped the driver. This could be a movie script." I added, reading a bit further.

Her fingers went to her mouth. She shook her head, "Oh my... the poor guard... what was his name... Anthony Rosario... he was beat up."

"The female guard... handcuffed."

We both read quietly for a few seconds. After the heist, the female guard somehow managed to undo her bonds and get help. Some of the money was retrieved, but not all.

"Wait a minute. Look at this." Sarah pointed to a paragraph at the bottom of the screen.

Anthony Rosario, the Brinks' driver was found to have connections with the mafia. He was arrested, found guilty and sentenced to twenty years. Two other accomplices were also found guilty of the crime. The three claimed no knowledge of what happened to the missing three million dollars.

"Exactly half," I mused. "Like it was an even split."

"Yeah but maybe one of them decided to hide the money from the others, even from the mafia, and buried the three million somewhere!" She said excitedly.

She could be right. Not about the buried treasure part, of course. Jeb Masurki must have been referring to the missing three million when he confronted me. So, he at least, didn't think someone in the mafia took the money.

"Sarah, I got something to tell you, but you can't tell anyone else, okay?"

She pretended to zipper her lips. Sealed shut on this issue. Good enough for me.

"A few days ago, some guy nearly ran me over. Then he jumped out his car and pushed me around."

"Jeez, Billy."

I pointed to yesterday's paper, opened to the article about Jeb Mazurki's death.

"This was the guy."

Her eyes widened.

"Wait, there's something else. When he roughed me up, he said something about Gramps having the money."

She stared at me, eyes wide. "Your granddad was involved?"

I shook my head furiously to stop her from thinking and verbalizing such a possibility.

"No," I replied immediately too loudly. I didn't care and I didn't look up. No whispers now.

"This Jeb guy just said that Gramps had better give him his share. But, really, my grandfather... he can't be involved. It just doesn't make sense."

She looked at me with her eyebrows pinched together. Then looked down at the article. "Yeah, I understand. You're probably right. Stupid idea. He wasn't involved." The bell rang and she got up.

We walked into the hallway with students laughing and talking as everyone migrated to their respective classes. My mind shifted between the wild cowboy and the old man in a flannel shirt who sorted coins. Sorting coins which he referred to as dollars into equal piles. A flash of insight seared my brain and all the pieces to the puzzle lined up perfectly. Gramps had to be involved.

Students trickled into one room or another, but I stopped and put my head against a locker. Though Gramps became a responsible husband and father, the wild young man was always inside. I felt Sarah's hand on my back. I turned and faced her.

"He was a pretty crazy when he was young. He bragged about how he once jumped from his horse onto a steer in the middle of a stampede. Dad never believed it, but Gramps insisted it was true. Even when he got married and settled down, he had this crazy streak in him. My grandmother called him the 'Wild Texan.' And, he had some gambling debts which were erased around the time of the robbery. Sarah, he could have been involved."

She touched my sleeve, pressing gently on my arm. "I think he had to be."

From behind me I heard a voice.

"You still teaching her chemistry, Taylor?" It was Rick and there were no smiles this time. He pushed me against the locker.

"Little too cozy, asshole. She's mine. Got it?"

Sarah tried to push him away, but a human mountain is hard to move. "I don't belong to you or anybody, Rick Henson. Leave him alone."

I was startled by Rick, but not afraid. When I was bullied by someone in seventh grade my Dad found out and took me into the garage.

*

Dad had placed a large, thick mat on the garage floor.

"Son, you fight someone, either you or the other guy gets hurt. Trust me. It always ends up bad."

I looked up at him. I couldn't figure out what he meant. "So, I don't fight? I just run away."

He smiled. "You never run away, Bill. But it's okay to let the person fight himself."

I had no idea what he meant.

He stood up. "Take a swing at me. Try to hit my face."

"Huh?"

"Hit me, Bill. Take a punch."

I shrugged and took a swing. Dad didn't block the punch. He grabbed my arm and a second later, I was on the ground.

He towered above me.

"You know karate, Dad?"

"Nope. Called judo. Karate is from Korea. Judo is from Japan. First letter of each gives a clue where it came from."

After helping me up, he taught me judo. We practiced and practiced for over two weeks. I learned how to use someone else's aggression and strength against themselves.

When I finally confronted my bully, I didn't punch him, but deflected his punches and threw him to the ground each time. He finally got too tired and frustrated. The bully, Joe, ended up as my best friend.

*

Rick's large hands gripped my shoulder as he pressed me against the locker. Using one of the judo maneuvers, I pushed Rick away. He tried to hold on, but only succeeded in ripping my shirt pocket off. I hoped that would be the end of it, but then his fist fired out at me. Instead of blocking the punch, I tilted my head away, caught the arm and pulled him forward, my leg outstretched to trip him. He fell and his head moved toward the locker. In control, I pulled him away from a collision with hard metal and wrapped his other arm behind him. I ended up straddling his back, pinning him down. Underneath me, he was breathing hard and tried to get up but I twisted the arm I was holding. He winced in pain and stopped struggling.

I leaned in toward his ear. "I don't want to fight, Rick. Let's quit this okay?"

He tried again to get up and I applied more pressure. Rick's eyes closed shut with the pain. Breathing heavily, he shook his head in agreement. That was when the vice-principal yanked me off his back.

CHAPTER NINE

"Sit down!"

Rick and I dropped onto hard, armless chairs in front of the Vice Principal. Mr. Minx was about my height. Looking at his hard face, I wondered if it had been chiseled out of granite with facial lines frozen in the frown position. In fact, I had never seen even the hint of a smile on his face. A former football coach, he makes habitually tardy students do push-ups as a punishment. We were in for much worse.

His eyes settled on Rick. "So, what was all this about, young man?"

Rick just shook his head, looking down. The piercing stare switched to me.

"Who started the fight..." he looked down at a file on his desk, "... Taylor?"

I looked over at Rick. He was just slowly shaking his head, his eyes closed. Apparently, when he started pushing me around in the hall, he had forgotten the first game of the season was Saturday night. Well, if playing ostrich works for Henson, it should work for me too. So I lowered my eyes and mimicked Rick's head motion.

Minx was apparently used to such reactions from students. The usual punishment for fights was the suspension of one or both of the students. All I heard was some papers being shuffled about on his desk. "All right, since both of you were fighting I'm afraid that both of you..."

I sighed and momentarily closed my eyes. There are times when I am my worst enemy.

"I pulled him to the ground and held him down." I said quickly before Minx could finish.

I raised my eyes to Minx. He stared at me, his pen tapping on some form. I was my mother's child so I stared right back at him.

"You're sure that's what happened?"

I sighed and nodded.

Minx didn't seem happy, but, of course, he never does. My peripheral vision noted that Rick's head was up, looking at me, probably delighted I was such an idiot. The Vice Principal looked at Rick.

"That what happened Rick?"

There was a delay of a few seconds. My stomach turned somersaults. I looked over to Rick and he stared back at me as he answered. "He's telling the truth, Mr. Minx."

"Either of you going to tell me why?"

Simultaneously our heads dropped to study the floor. There was silence for a few more seconds. Actually, I didn't think Minx really believed what I told him. I mean you just had to look at the two of us to realize it would be suicide for me to take on the six foot-three, two hundred pound quarterback. Then I recalled the pictures hanging in his office. Autographed pictures from a few pro football players; a larger picture, much older, of a group of mud drenched high school football players, all smiling, holding up a football. I grunted and shook my head. I gave him a great deal at a bargain price. A quick fix and a star quarterback playing Saturday. Sometimes people believe too easily.

The Vice-Principal nodded. He signed one paper and pushed the other one to the side.

"All right, Mr. Taylor call your... ahh..." opened the folder again. "... mother and have her come here to pick you up. Suspension, three days. Rick I don't know what's behind all this, but you have to lead by example, young man. You can go now." In a second, Rick was gone.

Minx stared at me for a few seconds and I got uncomfortable and looked away. I knew my role in this: I was the sacrificial lamb.

He gave me a pat lecture on the evils of fighting. Looking down at the patterns on the linoleum, I half-listened while he spouted off one platitude after another. Three days suspension seemed rather excessive to me. I mean I wasn't hitting Rick; I was just trying to hold him down so he wouldn't beat the crap out of me. And then he gets off with absolutely no penalty. I expected at least a detention or two. Or even three.

The secretary stuck her head in the door and announced the arrival of my mother. Minx got up and knocked the folder to the floor. Some papers slipped it out. As he scurried to pick them up, I saw the heading of one. It was a roster of students for one of the lunch periods. What was that doing in my folder, I wondered?

After he left the room to meet Mom, I leaned out of my chair and looked at the name on the folder. It wasn't my folder at all. It was headed Lunch Schedules. So, why was he looking in that folder and pretending to get information about me?

A few moments later Mom stormed into the room and sat down in the chair vacated by Rick. Minx brought out an entirely different folder that had my name clearly printed on the front. I registered the oddity somewhere in my brain, but right now an angry Mom held center stage in my brain.

When we were finally dismissed, she hurried out of school so I had to jog to keep up with her. Mom's silence scared me more than any hysterical screams. She got into the car and slammed the door. I took a deep breath and entered the cramped metal coffin. After we drove about a mile, she squeezed out a single question between clenched teeth. "Now, what the hell was going on?"

I told her the whole story starting with Sarah meeting me in the library and how Rick accosted me.

"I didn't want to fight, Mom" I mumbled, staring out the passenger window. "I just felt like I was trapped. And I remembered what Dad used to say about how I shouldn't ever start a fight, but I should defend myself." I felt a lump form in my throat when I thought of my Dad, I closed my eyes, determined that the tears welling in my eyes wouldn't be seen by my mother. I coughed to clear my throat.

"And then, he tried to punch me. I used the judo Dad taught me. It was like I was on auto pilot."

"Did you explain that to the vice-principal?"

I continued to look out of the window. I wasn't sure how she would handle this next part. I gulped and continued.

"Well, not all of it. I'm new here. Rick is, like, the most important person on the football team, and their first home game is Saturday. Everyone talks about winning the sectionals and their first game is with last year's sectional champs. He was about ready to suspend us both. If I dragged him down, the team would have lost. I was going to be suspended anyway, so I figured I might as well take most of the blame."

While we drove up the hill toward Gramp's house, I sneaked a peak at her. Her body wasn't as tense. She looked out her window for a moment.

"I think this Rick character is a coward and if he ever crosses my path..."

"Mom, I don't think you have to worry about that. It's not like the most popular guy in the school is ever going hang out at my house."

As we walked into the house, she put her arm around me and gave me a hug.

"You're a pretty good kid. You know that?"

I was embarrassed whenever she hugged me, but this time I leaned into the hug. It was great to have her on my side especially when my world was falling down all around me.

A playful smirk formed on my mom's face as she nudged me. "Except when you're beating up people." I couldn't suppress the smile. She tousled my hair like she used to do when I was a kid.

When we got inside we saw Mr. Songor talking with Gramps. Nice as Mr. Songor was, Gramps always got nervous when neither of us was around.

"Thanks, Kenny," said Mom with a smile. "You are, as ever, a godsend."

He smiled as he patted Gramps on the shoulder.

"Take care, Pete."

Mr. Songor turned to me, his face puzzled. I was never home this early.

"Bill, you all right?"

"Not doing all that great, Mr. Songor. Three day suspension."

He put his arms around my shoulders, like Dad used to do and walked me to the door.

"Fight or trouble with a teacher?"

"Fight."

"Truth be told, I was suspended once or twice in high school too. Happens to the best of us." He smiled at me. A moment later his face was more serious. He looked over to Mom who was fussing with Gramps and whispered to me.

"Hey, did you tell your Mom about that guy who nearly ran you over?"

"Yeah. Police came over to take a statement. But, did you see the news last yesterday? He was murdered!"

"No!"

"Yeah. It was also in the paper this morning."

"Drug related?"

"Maybe, but he was also part of some armored car robbery twenty years ago."

"Well, you know what they say… you play with fire, you're gonna get burned."

"Yeah. Kinda scary, though. I mean him being dead and all."

"It happens sometimes, Billy. It happens."

"Yeah. I guess."

He gave me a two-fingered salute and walked across the road to his home. I closed the door and recalled Minx's strange behavior. He already knew my name and that Mom was who I should contact. Did he know Dad was dead and that we were living with Gramps? Why pretend to be looking up the information in a bogus folder? What was that all about? Just another stupid thing about Conaroga. God, I hated this hole.

An hour later I took Gramps for a walk. He was happy when he could walk into his woods. He would mumble about this tree or that bush, sometimes he even identified them correctly. As we walked back to the cabin he turned to me. "Thanks for the walk, Billy."

He was about as lucid as he ever was and, for a moment, I was happy. A few steps later and he was staring blankly at the ground. The moment was gone. I linked my arm in his to make sure he didn't fall. I held him a little closer than I normally did.

Mom stayed home from work, "just in case." Later that evening, the three of us were finishing some left-overs, when we were interrupted by a knock at the door. I pushed my chair back and started to get up, but Mom motioned for me to sit back down. She was in her mother bear mode. It was probably Mr. Songor, but it could be, let's see, the vice principal, the police, either from Conaroga or Rochester, the lawyer, or maybe even Sarah. It was none of the above. Mom opened the door a crack so I couldn't see the person. But, she wasn't smiling.

"Come in." she said flatly.

The tall form of Rick Henson emerged through the door. And, he didn't look happy.

CHAPTER TEN

I quickly rose and stepped away from the table, ready for anything. Mom helped Gramps from the table and eased him into his chair by the fire, the coins all mixed up again. Rick stood directly in front of me. This was almost the same confrontational positions from earlier in the day. He realized he was standing too close so he stepped back. The guy's face was strained like he tasted something bad and wanted to spit it out. I waved him to a chair.

He slumped down. Mom stood between the kitchen and the living room so she could watch Gramps and us. When Rick looked up at her, he got the 'stare.' He quickly looked away. His bravado, so apparent in school, was entirely gone. Finally he looked up to me, took a deep breath, and began.

"I didn't feel right about what I did today. Ya know… not telling Minx about me starting it. It's just that… well, the game, me being the quarterback and all." His forehead wrinkled, the look now clear to me. Rick Henson had a conscience. "It was a lousy thing that I did… or didn't do. I mean, I should have told Minx I started it." He braved a glance toward Mom and retreated a moment later. No absolution there.

He stared at the floor for a moment and took a deep breath, like he was going under water for a deep dive. When he looked at me again, the pent up air burst out forming words. "What you did... hey, that was something, man." I said nothing. Rick looked away and then stood up.

"Anyway I'm sorry." He put out his hand. I wasn't sure what he was sorry about... being a jerk, starting the fight, or not telling Minx what really happened, but I guess it didn't matter.

I kept my stony expression while I shook his hand.

He nodded, waited a moment, maybe expecting me to say something. Last year's all-county quarterback shrugged and walked back toward the front door. He opened it to go out, but paused for a moment and looked back.

"I... uhh... I went back to Minx and told him what really happened." He sounded a mirthless chuckle and continued. "Still didn't get suspension. Said I did the right thing and felt I had learned my lesson. But I have detention all next week. I tried man."

My sole acknowledgement was my head barely dipping down and then back up. I doubted it would change my suspension status. The deck was too stacked against me. Rick mumbled goodbye and left.

Mom had walked back to the sink and finished washing the plates. "Well, I give him credit for trying, at least. Far as I'm concerned he's off the hook." She harrumphed. "Besides, he's too busy kicking himself for me to do anything."

I sat with Gramps. All right, I thought, Rick did the right thing. Nevertheless, I remained pissed. Really pissed. How can you properly hate someone when he admitted he's wrong and tried to fix it? Besides being obnoxious, far too popular, Sarah's boyfriend and a certified idiot, he was also grossly unfair. The least he could have done was to leave me with my anger. Damn it! I didn't want to like the guy. But, I did. Only a little, though.

I focused on the old man carefully separating coins, and my mind drifted back to the robbery. Was coin counting a repeat of something else which happened over twenty years ago? A memory Gramps was desperately holding on to? Was he involved with the heist? I sat down to watch some TV. Sometimes it's best not to think about things.

On Friday, Mom took a double shift. Fortunately, she was a terrific nurse, and the local hospital happily gave her a green light to work overtime.

I got granddad up, and helped with his morning routine: brushing his teeth, getting dressed and fixing him breakfast. After he settled down in front of the TV to watch some nature show, I researched the robbery on the net. Mostly I focused on the life and times of the bogus security guard, Anthony Rosario. He was connected to the mob so he must have been the mastermind.

A picture taken around the time of the crime showed a grinning man with a swarthy complexion and dark, wavy hair. He could have been a supporting actor in any of the mafia movies past or present. The picture of him leaving prison showed him worn down with age and confinement.

Neither picture prepared me for his violent background. He was accused of so many crimes I didn't even bother to count them. I did count the number of murder indictments, however: four. But he was cleared of every single one. Now I understood the cocky smile in the first picture. In fact, the only charge which stuck to him was a jewelry store robbery in his teens when he was caught with the missing jewels in his pocket. He got out in one year with good behavior. There was no such break with the armored car robbery. It wouldn't surprise me if he had something to do with Jeb's death.

Saturday was the first really cold day of autumn, but there wasn't a cloud in the sky. Mom was taking a bath so I had to monitor Gramps. Instead of playing with his coins, he walked from the living room, through the kitchen and to the front door. Then he would turn around and walk back.

"Nice day." Gramps said looking out the front door window.

"Yup." I answered. I was trying to get our antique modem to the imm-imm-imm noise which means it connected to the internet. Instead all I got was nah-nah-nahhh.

"Let's walk, Billy. Let's walk."

I pushed the start button again on the computer and waited, fingers crossed.

"Just wait a minute, Gramps."

"Nice day, we should walk."

The internet finally connected, just as Gramps opened the door.

Crap!

"Wait, Granddad!"

I held his arm while he strained to go outside.

"We'll go out. Just let me get your coat on, okay?"

I helped Gramps with his coat, zippering it for him. I may have been a bit too rough because he looked at me strangely. When he looked at the storm door, his face erupted with a great smile. He pulled me slowly toward the door. I took one last look at the miraculous internet connection and clenched my jaw. All I could think about was how Gramps messed up my morning. I finally gave up all hope of internet surfing, even with the crap system we had. I grabbed his arm, and led him through the door.

"Come on. Let's go on this damn walk."

I took him for a walk around the house, hoping it would placate him and we could go back inside quickly. No such luck. He kept pointing to the woods. I sighed and we slowly trudged to the trees and the bushes that reminded him so much of Letchworth Park.

Half an hour later when we finally emerged from the woods, I saw Sarah's Mustang in the driveway. Frustrated with his slow, careful steps, I pulled him along as fast as I could. He stumbled a few times and I didn't care. Now it was my turn.

CHAPTER ELEVEN

When I helped Gramps inside, I heard my mom and Sarah laughing. I cringed, worried that Mom was telling stories about me when I was younger; she had a few choice ones which never failed to make me blush.

Gramps and I walked into the living room. Sarah turned toward us, and put her hands to her mouth to stifle her laughter.

"Well, hello William," she said and both woman laughed. My head sank to my chest in utter defeat. Mom must have shared the story about how I rejected the name Billy and insisted on being called William all the time. I was only four years old for Christ's sake! Looking up, I gave Mom a withering look, but they both just laughed harder.

After their laughter subsided Sarah linked her arm with Gramps.' His smile and Sarah's presence brightened the living room.

"Abby, so glad you came over. I missed you." Sarah tilted her head, hunched her shoulders, and gave an apologetic frown to Mom. Mom smiled and nodded. 'Abby' helped Gramps with his coat, and I got the coins out for him. She patted him on the arm and walked back into the kitchen. When I was done spreading the coins, I looked up to see them whispering together, Sarah giggling.

"Come on. Enough already." I whined.

Both broke into gales of laughter. Mom came over to hug me and that was so uncool. I tried to shrug her off, but unsuccessfully.

Time to divert the conversation.

"Why does Gramps call Sarah your name, Mom?"

Mom finally let me go. "It's our hair."

That made no sense whatsoever as mom was a short-haired brunette with a few gray strands hinting at her age, and Sarah's hair was soft, blond and much longer. Slightly curly. There were these strands which encircled her ear perfectly. And also... well, Sarah's hair was different. Also Sarah was shorter than me, and Mom was my height.

Mom went to the hall closet, reached up high, and pulled out an album. Setting the worn, blue photobook on the table she motioned for us to sit beside her. Thumbing through far too many pictures of me she finally turned to an old photo showing Dad and I dressed up for some rock climbing. "That's Bill's dad."

Sarah giggled. "Cute helmet."

I was annoyed because I did look goofy in the helmet. It was a size too large. I had begged Dad to let me go without it. "It was a state law or something," I grumbled.

Mom then turned to a much younger version of herself beside Dad. She was completely blond and with hair even longer than Sarah's.

"When I first met your Dad I was a blond. I've dyed my hair brunette ever since." She joked. Mom looked at the picture longer than either Sarah or I. She wiped a tear from her face.

Gently caressing the picture with her finger tip, she closed the album, and got up. "Well, enough of this. I have to go shopping." I was about to ask her what stores were open this early, when I saw her wink at me. Oh, so she was playing matchmaker now.

When she came out of her bedroom with her purse and pulling her coat on, I just rolled my eyes at her. A minute later she was gone. I figured I had to change subject quickly again.

"That's my Mom. She sure does love shopping. Well, what did I miss in school?"

Sarah plopped on the couch beside me and briefly explained a few techniques in math, gave me some worksheets from history, and a small packet which was a short story from English.

"Mr. Sneal was out yesterday, so we didn't do anything new in chemistry."

She focused those two blue eyes on me. My stomach danced whenever she looks at me that way.

"Rick told me what happened in Minx's office. How you took the blame. He feels terrible about what he did, Billy."

"He should feel terrible." I responded, my face not moving.

She looked out the window for a moment. She kept staring outside when she spoke.

"Give him a chance, Billy."

I nodded, not knowing what to say. I probably would give him a 'chance', but that was between me and Rick. I didn't like Sarah trying to patch things up between the golden boy and me.

The entire review of the day was done in five minutes. I took the books to my room. When I returned I saw her looking at the laptop on the table. Amazingly, the connection to the internet remained working in the hour since I had gotten it to work.

"I've been trying to find out more information about the robbery," I explained. I tapped into a recent favorite site about the robbery. "Apparently a gray van was seen following the stolen armored car. Read here."

She read the passage I had pointed out. "A shoot-out in Avondale?"

"Yeah. Some guy got killed, too. He was part of the mafia."

She kept reading, biting her finger.

"Three million was found in the van, huh?"

"Yup."

She looked at me, bubbling with excitement. "So, there is..."

"... three million missing," I finished.

"Yes," she said with two hands tightly folded above her heart, "the buried treasure." I wasn't sure if she really believed that or if she was baiting me.

"Stop with the 'buried treasure', Sarah."

"Where is the three million then, Billy?"

"M-a-f-i-a," I spelled out.

"J-e-b."

"Whatta you mean?"

"He was looking for it."

"Yeah. So?"

"He's dead now." She answered.

"Drug related."

She rolled her eyes. "Why can't you see the obvious?"

I didn't answer.

She pointed back to the article. "Avondale, where the shootout was, is between us and Rochester. Not too far away."

"Once again... so what?"

"The three million could be buried in Avondale or even around here."

Somehow Sarah's speculation about a buried treasure had morphed into a fact. Now she forced me to consider where it might be buried!

"Sarah…" I started but Gramps mumbled something and we both listened.

"Ten thousand in this pile, ten thousand over there. Need more over there."

We both looked at each other and then at Gramps, but he was quiet again.

"Has he ever said that before?" She asked whispering in my ear.

"No. It's always been a 'dollar here, dollar there.' "

Sarah's blue eyes were wider than ever. "Everything fits, Billy. Gramps separated the money and then buried it somewhere."

I thought for a moment. If Gramps secreted away the missing three million, it would explain quite a bit. How granddad miraculously got out of debt. Jeb intercepting me. How the van ended up in Avondale. Finally, it might explain granddad's obsession with counting money. Especially with this 'ten thousand' sorting thing.

"Maybe," I conceded. "He was a park ranger then."

I involuntarily shuddered. Damn it! Why did I say 'maybe' about the buried treasure?

"Then the money must be buried in the park." Concluded Sarah. I frowned.

"Whoa. Not buried, not in the park." I insisted.

"But, you just said…"

"Sarah stop. Think about it."

Sarah put her hands on her hips. It wasn't going to be easy to change her mind.

"Lotta speculation here, girl. If that is the way he paid off the debt, if he really did bury it, if he buried it in Letchworth, if the mafia never dug it up. If-if-if-if."

Sarah looked hurt. "It could be true."

"Well, we won't find out what really happened on the internet. The crooks haven't uploaded their thoughts on the matter. Until then, it's just missing money with no story." I chuckled.

She looked at me for a moment, and a sly smile crept across her face. I was worried.

"Sarah, what are you thinking about now?"

She got up from the table and patted me on the hand. "Oh, nothing to do with Jeb. But, I have to go now. Gotta get back to shop with my Mom. Wouldn't it be funny if we met up with your Mom?"

"Yeah, hilarious."

She put her coat on and I opened the door for her.

"Hey, thanks for coming over. You know, giving me all the work and stuff."

Sarah laughed. "It's fun giving you work... William."

I shook my head, but grinned at her.

She stopped at the door. "Bill, you're right. We can't get anything more out of the internet."

She looked up at me with a big smile.

"But, maybe we can get some information from Hank Patterson."

Then she bounced down the front steps toward her car.

I knew who he was. Last night I had read in another article that Hank Patterson, Jeb, and Anthony Rosario were the three guys who served time in prison for the robbery.

"Yeah, he was the third guy." I said from the doorway.

Then I thought for a moment. The article we had been reading only mentioned Anthony Rosario.

"Hey, how did you know?"

She raised her eyebrows, gave me a faint smile and got into her car.

"How did you know this guy's name?" I started down the steps after her. Gramps called me and I stopped. Sarah closed her car door shut, but the window slid down when I backed up the porch steps to return to Gramps.

"How did I know Patterson's name?" she yelled. "My Dad told me. He's our neighbor's husband."

CHAPTER TWELVE

I fixed a turkey sandwich for granddad while I grumbled about Sarah's abrupt departure; I wish she would have stayed just a bit longer and explained a lot more. After gobbling down the meal Gramps stood by the door. Once again I put his coat back on him and out we went. I loosely held his arm, letting him choose the path and, of course, he shuffled right toward the woods behind his cabin. I felt bad about how I treated him this morning. I shouldn't blame him about the miserable place I found myself.

A dense forest touches the back part of his property, and I gently directed him away from the thorny bushes and the brambles as we entered it. Thinking he was in Letchworth Park, Gramps went on about how he cleared out some thick weeds so folks could use one of the hiking paths. He stopped and looked around, a puzzled look on his face. "Not here. Not here."

"What, Gramps? What's not here?"

"Not here, Billy. Not anymore."

I kept asking him, but he just shook his head and went back to holding my arm for support while we walked over the rough terrain. He often said crazy stuff like this. Now, however, I wasn't so sure it was "crazy." Was he talking about Sarah's "buried treasure"?

Later in the afternoon, Mom returned home after her shopping trip.

"So, how did it go with Sarah?"

"Fine, good...I dunno she stayed for about an hour then she left. No big deal." Mom raised an eyebrow and continued to stare at me. She wanted more information, of course, but sharing with Mom the relationship I had with Sarah (whatever it was) was not on the top of my list for discussion items. But the pregnant silence demanded some filler.

"She had to go shopping with her mom. Besides, the game's tonight. She's a cheerleader."

"Did you ask her for a date?"

"Jeez, Mom. You don't ask someone for a date anymore. You hang out with them. Besides, she's already got a boyfriend. Remember?"

She raised her eyebrows. "Rick Henson? You're so much better than he is, Bill. Sarah's a smart girl. Call her. Make a date or hang out with her or whatever. She'll say yes. Trust me."

You don't argue with Mom when she has her mind set. So I didn't even try. Instead, I got on my sneakers and went out for a run, a long, serious run. It kept me in shape and it also gave me some alone time to think. And I had a bunch to think about. Not just my status with Sarah, but also Gramps' possible involvement with the biggest Brinks' robbery ever.

During supper Mom hinted at how nice it would be for me to "just go out and have some fun." The game was the one place I would have considered, but because of my suspension I wasn't allowed on school property. Exaggerating a few yawns, I retreated to my room. Better to pretend being sleepy than tell Mom the truth about not being able to attend school functions when you're suspended. If she knew, there was no telling where her anger would take us.

Granddad was snoring peacefully in the next bed. I lay down on my bed with my arms behind my head. I wasn't sleepy yet and, even if I was, it was doubtful I could sleep through the bass symphony Gramps provided.

Maybe Mom was right about Sarah. She was angry with Rick and not just about the fight. Maybe she would consider hanging out with me. We seemed to enjoy each other's company. A movie. We could go to a movie together. She had talked about the horror flick at the multiplex. Might have been a hint.

I looked at the clock. By now she should be cheering one of Rick's touchdowns, I thought glumly. Might be a good time to call her cell phone; she certainly wouldn't answer during the game and I wouldn't get tongue-tied. I thought about what I might say. "Look, I know you're busy, but what about... " Yeah, that might work. Short and sweet. No pressure. I could pull this off, I was sure. I wish my tumbling stomach would agree. I took my cell phone out of my pocket and dialed her number praying she wouldn't pick up. I breathed a sigh of relief when I got her voice mail.

"Hi, Sarah. Hey, if you want to see that new movie about, you know, the end of the world, zombies and stuff... the one with Emily Stone, well, I was thinking of seeing it Sunday night, and if you wanted to see it I thought, maybe, we could see it together. You know a date. Umm. It would be my treat. I mean I would pay. So, don't worry about that..."

I hung up.

"Crap!" What an idiot! I just rambled on. And, I called it a date. Thanks, Mom, for putting that notion in my head. Great plan, Taylor. Great delivery.

I should have texted her. I thought about texting her now, but that was so lame. Calling her up, stupid, and then texting her, desperate.

Unable to sleep, I listened to the second half of the game on the local radio station. Conaroga High won and Rick scored three touchdowns. I waited for a half hour after the game, but no call from Sarah. At least I understood why she didn't call me back after my stupid phone call. I slipped under the covers and let sleep dim the image of Sarah hanging on the arm of Rick Henson... National Honor Society - Football Hero.

I rose late Sunday morning, feeling sorry for myself. Granddad was getting up and I angrily swung out of bed. Had to help with Gramps so I got him and myself ready for another dull day. Mom beamed brighter than the sunlight streaming in through the window.

"Hi, honey, how was your night?"

Annoyed that she seemed insensitive to my foul mood, I snapped at her.

"Oh, great Mom. Let's see, I cleaned up Gramps 'cause he can't do it himself anymore. Then I laid on my bed since there's nothing else to do. Oh, I did listen to the game on the radio and Rick Henson, Sarah's boyfriend, you know the one I'm so much better than, well he scored three touchdowns. Good for him. Good for Sarah since she cheered each one. Great night, just great."

She was silent as she put blueberry pancakes in front me, real blueberries, and I realized I was a certified jerk. Gramps wasn't the reason I was upset and the rest of what I said was just cheap shots. I was upset because I am such an incompetent dweeb when it comes to girls. I pushed the pancake around the plate.

"I'm sorry, Mom."

She put her hand on my shoulder. "I know taking care of Gramps isn't easy. But, we do what we have to do."

"It's not Gramps. It's other things."

"Like what?" she asked waving the red cape. I exploded again.

"Like I want to go back to Florida, Mom. I don't like it here. I don't fit in."

Mom went back to the sink, her back to me, busying herself with the dishes. Her body was as rigid as two inch thick piece of oak plank. Her words, however, came out soft and understanding.

"I know it was unfair to you, Billy. But, we had to do it."

Before I could dig my hole any deeper, Gramps shuffled into the kitchen. "Pancakes, Abby? Pancakes. Yum."

He sat down smiling at me. He was a pain, but when he was in a good mood... well, you just felt better somehow. "I'll get some for you, Gramps."

I got a plate for him. Mom stayed at the sink, her shoulders slumping down, chin to her chest over the sink. She was taking a long time to clean the sink. I stepped behind her.

"Mom, I'm sorry. Again."

She said nothing, but she wiped her nose with her sleeve. Great. Suspended, no girlfriend, no friends at all (I refused to count Jerry as a friend when I was in this mood), and I've succeeded in making my mother cry. Another banner day for William Taylor.

When Mom finally finished scrubbing the sink, she saw my full plate, and ordered me to eat my pancakes. With granddad slopping pancakes into his mouth and Mom bossing me around what passed for normalcy returned to the cabin.

After she cleared the plates off the table, she studied me. I looked away, momentarily closing my eyes. A lecture was coming.

"Billy, you've got to give this town a chance. Part of the problem is you. If you don't make an effort to get out with your friends, you don't have a chance here because you don't give yourself a chance. In fact, Sarah is the only the friend you've ever invited to the house. I'm home all day, so why don't you call up somebody else and do something with them."

I bit my tongue hard, stood up and looked at frost on the ground, just now glistening as it melted. I didn't want to tell Mom I had no friends. This early morning brush fire would turn into a raging forest fire if I told her the truth. So, I simply pushed the problem to later.

"Maybe you're right, Mom. I think I'll first just go for a run this morning. Then I'll try to catch up with someone. Gotta catch up on some school work too."

Mom tilted her head and scrutinized me with narrowed eyes. That I capitulated so quickly made her suspicious. She knows me too well. Her mouth opened to say something when a knock at the door diverted her attention. She opened the door for Mr. Songor. He patted me on the back.

"Hey, Billy boy. How ya doing, buddy?"

Before I could answer, Mom chimed in. "I'm trying to push him out of the house today." She put some pancakes in front of Mr. Songor who protested, then smelled the steam, tilted his head, and smiled. He grabbed for the maple syrup.

Between mouthfuls, Mr. Songor looked at me. "Your Mom's right. You gotta get out more, William."

"Yeah, maybe."

"He has a new friend." Mom said, "A girlfriend. I'm trying to get him to ask her out."

"Mom, seriously, drop it. Sarah's just a friend, not a girlfriend." The more I protested the more they smiled. I stomped back to my room. It was rarely a fair fight with Mom

92

but with two of them hounding me, there was no hope. Retreat was my only option. My phone was still on the charger. There were three missed calls. I still get a few calls from my friends in Florida, so I figured it was one of them. I clicked the first message.

"Hi, Billy. Hey, did you hear we won!" It was Sarah. There was laughter in the background and the line went dead.

I grunted. Great. Just great.

Second message. Nothing, just dead air. Third message, garbled but it didn't sound like anyone from Florida. I could make out the words "money" and "stop." But, it made no sense. My phone seemed to be a magnet for telemarketers. Fortunately, the poor reception in the back-water county rendered most of them garbage like this last message. I deleted all three messages.

I checked my text messages. There were two from Sarah.

Movie? Can't tonight.

I looked out the window, shaking my head. I knew the sword was coming down. At least she didn't say 'What? Are you kidding me?' Well, that was that. I guess I was still kinda of hoping she might say "sure" or something like that. I sighed, thought about deleting the second message but opened it up anyway.

Matinee? Munch at my house after. B4 movie U&I have mission. CU @ noon.

I just smiled and smiled and smiled again, ready to do the big "Whoopee!" but screaming might freak out Mom and Mr. Songor. I strolled into the kitchen, grabbed an apple, tossed it in the air, and took a great bite out of it. Apples were the one thing New York got right.

Between chews I managed to slop out: "Hey guys, I think I'm going to the movies after all."

"Oh you are, are you?" Mom replied with a coy smile, "Need a ride?"

"Nope, I'm good." I said just before taking another bite.

"Who's taking you?"

"Ahh... Sarah."

Mr. Songor put his head down, a smile across his face while he stared at the wisps of steam rising from his coffee. Mom folded her arms. "Sarah, huh? Your friend who just happens to be a girl."

I just closed my eyes, turned around, suffered the stifled laughter and walked into the bathroom to get ready.

CHAPTER THIRTEEN

When Sarah stepped inside the house, she ignored me, greeted Mom who was finishing the dishes and went over to Gramps. He interrupted his "work" for a second with a smile. She patted him on the shoulder and returned to the kitchen. Mom asked Sarah about the movie and, upon hearing it was a horror flick, scrunched her face and shook her head. Mom was strictly a romantic-comedy type of woman.

When we got into the car I finally got a chance to exchange words with my friend who was a girl. "All right, Ms. Seeley, what's up?"

She grinned as she turned out of the driveway. "I thought we might pay a visit to Mrs. Patterson."

"The wife of the third guy?"

"Yup, she might know some of the pieces to the puzzle. I visit her once a week just to say hello. She doesn't have many friends and I thought she had no husband."

"I don't know Sarah. If her husband is there..."

"Don't be a wuss. He won't be there. She doesn't even wear a ring, so what does that tell you? It's been twenty years for heaven's sake."

"I'm not so sure, Sarah."

"Geez, Billy, you sound just like my Dad. He says I shouldn't visit her anymore."

"I agree with your dad. Three million dollars missing and one murder. Not a good combination."

"Come on, Billy. I know Mrs. Patterson. She's just a sweet, older lady who is lonely. If you don't want to talk about the buried money, that's all right. We'll just stop in to say hello."

I looked out the window. I knew I was beaten even before the battle began. I wanted to be with her too much. Out of the corner of my eye I caught her looking at me while I stared straight ahead. Made me nervous. Hoped I didn't have any food on my face. I looked back at her.

"Besides, Dad didn't think Mr. Patterson moved back." Then in a deeper voice, "But, just to be on the safe side no more visits to old lady Patterson." I couldn't help but chuckle at her accurate imitation of her dad.

A few minutes later we drove past Sarah's house. Well, Sarah's houses. Apparently there was the main house and the smaller guest house with a four car garage between the two. As I saw more and more of the manicured lawn, winding driveway, and columned house, I slumped down into my seat. Opposite her entry way which, by the way, was flanked by two sculptured lions snarling at any visitor, she turned onto a gravel driveway. Old pine trees, interspersed with large bushes and thin saplings, partially blocked the view of the estate across the road.

A car pulled in behind us. I twisted around. The driver had a mass of white hair and looked like Old Tom, the school bus driver. Sarah drove her car around the bend and the car disappeared.

It had to be Old Tom, I concluded. What was he doing here? Following us? As I pondered the puzzle, Sarah's Mustang came to rest at the end of the gravel. A pair of thin paths, four feet apart and parallel, penetrated deeper into the woods. Tire tracks.

Sarah jumped out and walked quickly along one of the well-worn paths. I ran to catch up with her. She gave me no time to ask questions or abort the mission. Before we angled down into a hollow, I caught one last glimpse of her estate. In particular, her swimming pool and tennis court.

"Nice home, Sarah."

She reached for my hand to hurry me along. Her grasp was soft, but firm. I liked the feel of it.

"When we moved here a few years ago, my Dad kinda discouraged me from talking to Mrs. Patterson. The Harmons over there were fine to talk to, big house and all. But the little lady in the cottage..." She adopted a deeper tone which sounded like her father, "Best not to disturb her, honey."

I smiled. Sarah had an independent streak. Well, more than a streak, an independent alter ego.

"Mrs. Patterson was always nice to me. She rents the house. Works at the gas station at the edge of the village."

"Oh, I know her. Yeah, she is nice."

We reached a clearing in the dark woods. Beside the cottage was a red Volkswagen, one of the originals from the sixties. A few dents and a missing rear bumper attested to its age. Encircling the house was tall grass with a few wild flowers that stubbornly survived the frosty mornings. It would have been a perfect home for the witch in Hansel and Gretel. With that disconcerting thought stuck in my brain we climbed the rickety steps.

Sarah knocked. Mrs. Patterson opened the door and looked more haggard than I remembered her when I paid for Mom's gas two weeks ago. I realized then that make-up was not a frivolity; with some women it was an outright necessity. She smiled at us, looked over Sarah's shoulders, right and left, and then opened the door wide for us to enter.

After closing the front door, she looked at me. "And who is this fine, young man, Miss Sarah?"

Sarah extended her arm as though she was presenting some sort of act in a variety show. "This, Mrs. Patterson, is William Taylor, esquire."

"I've seen you around, young man and I have good feelings about you."

"I've been in the store a few times, Mrs. Patterson."

Wearing a faded yellow robe, she led us to her kitchen. It had a disturbingly large, black oven. She went to her cupboard and brought down some Oreo cookies and placed them in front of us. There was some idle chit-chat, but Mrs. Patterson was no dummy. I hadn't touched the plate and Sarah nibbled on a single cookie.

"Now, what brings you two over here? Certainly not the cookies."

Sarah looked at me sheepishly. Oh, so not only was I pushed to go on this ill-fated mission, I also had to lead the charge. I glared at Sarah, who smiled sweetly. I coughed.

"Well, Mrs. Patterson we… ah… I found out that your… ah… husband was… well…"

"… was involved in the Brinks robbery. Got arrested for it." Mrs. Patterson finished.

She closed her baggy eyes as she shook her head back and forth. When she opened her eyes she looked out the window.

"Dear Jesus, it's been a secret too long. Might as well tell someone."

She looked back at us.

"Hank had too many friends who made good money the bad way. So, he decided to 'step up in the world.' It was supposed to be the perfect crime."

A flat chuckle escaped her lips. "All three got arrested in two days." She got up and poured herself a cup of coffee. It was then that I saw the extra mug beside the coffee maker.

"Did your husband ever talk about what happened?" asked Sarah.

Mrs. Patterson looked down into the coffee. "No. Not before the robbery. After the robbery I knew something was wrong, but he didn't say anything then either. Then the police came."

The empty coffee cup made me nervous. I was pretty sure I knew what it meant. I started to get up. "Well, thanks, Mrs. Patterson. We'd better be going now."

Sarah gave me a stern look. I slowly settled back down.

"The police found three million dollars in a van." Sarah continued.

"Yeah, and no one found the other three million. Those three knuckleheads don't know where it is, I can tell you that."

A voice came from behind the curtain that separated the kitchen from the rest of the little house.

"That's about enough, Maude." Sarah was startled, but I just put my head down. A man emerged from the behind the curtain. He slumped down in the last chair at the kitchen table. We were all too close to each other.

Hank Patterson was short and muscular before he went to prison. His police picture showed a hard face, defiant. A much wider body settled itself into the seat beside his wife. A police picture would now show a thick pale neck and head with sagging bags under his eyes pulling the whole face down. He closed those eyes as though they had finally given up fighting gravity. A few moments of silence passed. Then, eyes still closed, Hank Patterson's mouth woke up.

"Kid, why you so interested in this?"

I didn't want anyone targeting Gramps so I quickly ad-libbed.

"We're doing a term paper. Researching the biggest Brinks' robbery ever."

He opened his eyes and turned toward his wife. "Hey, Maude, I'm gonna be written up in some kid's term paper."

The eyes closed again.

"Okay, okay. I'll tell you what I know. Ain't much, though."

His body heaved forward and he leaned on the table. Flat, eyes looked directly at me.

"Money hain't been found. I knowed the mafia was supposed to get about half. Some asshole in the mob messed that one up." He chuckled under his breath again and finally looked at me.

"Tony Rosario, a mafia guy, he planned it. The guy studied robberies. You know how most guys got caught?"

His face devoid of expression, Hank waited for an answer. I shook my head no.

"It's bank money. Feds know the serial numbers. Local store owners would check big bills for the numbers and, bingo, the guy would be caught. But, Tony, he's smart. He had someone outside the mob hide it. Wait a few years and people forget them numbers."

Sarah saw her first opportunity to get important information. "The person who buried the money, he must have been somebody the mafia trusted."

He turned slowly toward Sarah.

"What buried money?"

Sarah paled under his scrutiny and I understood why. When I was about eight, I was with my Dad, running through a part of the Everglades. I slipped and fell. A cotton-mouth snake had

100

raised its head and was staring at me. Looking at its eyes I was too frightened to move. Dad chased it away. Hanks' eyes reminded me of the snake's eyes: without soul and predatory.

Hank turned back to me. "What's she talking about... 'buried money'?"

Sarah was scared, but, to her credit, didn't back down.

"Who hid the rest of the money?"

His head whipped back to her.

"How would I know?" he snapped.

"Because you were there." Replied Sarah, her voice a few decibels louder. Apparently her anger trumped her fear. I looked back at the door. How fast could I get her out of here?

Hank took her statement right in stride and registered no offense. Maybe prison made him more compliant. I hoped so.

"First, the mafia people trust nothing and nobody 'cepting themselves. Mafia guy hid the money."

Sarah asked another question.

"So, the only mafia guy was Anthony Rosario?" He just stared at her for a moment. I didn't know if he was going to answer her or wrap his meaty hands around her neck. Finally he spoke.

"Some guy higher up in the mafia met with us the night before the heist. Forget his name. Just a guy with that wavy, wop hair. He was checking us out before the robbery and trying to scare the shit out of us. 'Don't do this, don't do that.'"

"What was your role?" I asked, hoping to shift the snake stare from Sarah.

"Me? I just robbed the truck. We... that's Jeb and I... tied up Tony. He was hired on as a guard months before. He was a wop, but he had balls, I'll give him that."

As he looked up to the ceiling, the concentric circles of flab around his neck unfolded and we saw far too much fat and lint. "We roughed him up a bit." He grunted out what may have been his version of a chuckle. "Jesus, he looked at us bad when we was doing it. But, it had to look real, y'know? Anyway, I drove the Brinks' truck down into some woods just off the thruway. Gray van and my car was there. So was Big Shit and two other guys. One guy had a uniform on, but he wasn't a cop. Me and Jeb made sure Tony and the broad were tied up tight. Then we transferred the money to the van. Half of it in one bin, half in the other. The guy with the uniform helped us. Big Shit and Little Shit watched us like rats looking at an open garbage can. Afterwards, me and Jeb went back home. That's all."

"That's all you did?" asked Sarah.

He snorted. "Yeah, all I did. Got me twenty years."

"Why two bins?" I interjected.

He shrugged.

"Half of the take was for us, the other half for the mafia."

"The cops found three million and the rest of it was missing. Do you think... ahh... Big Shit and Little Shit hid the missing money?" I pressed.

"I told you already. Mafia didn't get their money. The mafia part was with them during the shoot-out in Avondale. Somebody else hid the other three million. Tony said it was some old crook in Rochester. Never gave a name."

"But he was a mafia guy?" Pressed Sarah.

Hank looked her. Then his face contorted. He may have been trying to think.

"Yeah. But maybe someone just connected with the mob. You know, someone who owed 'em money. Maybe. I dunno."

Now there was an edge to his voice. He wanted the interview to end and I was more than willing to accommodate him. I wanted to get away from this guy and the witch's house. "Thanks for the information, Mr. Patterson."

Sarah pulled me back down by the shirt when I started to get up again. "Wait, I have a few more questions."

"Damn, you broads are all alike... You ask too many questions."

"Shut-up, Hank. Maybe if you asked more questions you wouldn't have lost twenty years." Maude's voice was firm and angry.

"Could you describe the guy in the uniform?" Sarah was firing questions faster than a game show host on speed.

"Jesus, it was twenty years ago. It was dark green. He wasn't fat. Not tall either. Just normal looking. Jeb might tell you. He was fucking obsessed with getting the money back. It's all he talked about in Attica."

Apparently Hank didn't know that Jeb wasn't going to give us any information.

"Did Jeb ever talk about the guy in the green uniform?" asked Sarah.

He hesitated a moment, face strained, remembering.

"Yeah. Once. He remembered Big Shit calling the guy Pete."

CHAPTER FOURTEEN

We walked back to the car with me walking fast and Sarah moving far too casually, her face scrunched up. I kept looking over my shoulder.

"The guy in uniform... Gramps?" Sarah asked.

I shook my head and momentarily closed my eyes.

"You're right. Had to be Peter Taylor, my grandfather. Park rangers still wear dark green uniforms," I conceded.

"The guy who hid the money, Gramps?"

"No. I don't think so. Hank referred to an 'old crook' from Rochester. Gramps at the time of the robbery must have been... ahh... let's see... forty something. Not old."

"Also," I continued. "Gramps might have been a gambler, but not a crook. And, he didn't live in Rochester."

Sarah opened the door to her car. "Gramps was there, but didn't bury the money. Yet Jeb thought he had the money..."

She shook her head and looked at me across the top of her car.

"We're missing something. What role did your grandfather play?"

"I don't know about Gramp's role, but I know what we are missing. Our safety. Let's get out of here." I didn't think Hank had followed us. But, what about Old Tom? He must have been following us. Could he be hiding in the woods? The hairs on the back of my head stood up and I didn't know why. That worried me.

We got in the car. Sarah carefully backed up. I scanned all the windows while I talked.

"The shootout in Avondale was over the mob's three million dollars, I'm guessing. The other three million was hid."

"Uh-huh." Sarah agreed.

"Two mob guys. You know, Big and Little Crap. They must have been responsible for the mob's cut. Three million dollars."

She slowly nodded her head, agreeing with the logic.

"But, that was the money they found."

"So, the mob is out three million dollars. However..."

"I see where you are heading, Billy. The mob probably knew where the other three million was buried." finished Sarah.

"Yup," I repeated.

"So, you're thinking the mob grabbed the other money to make up for the loss?"

"Makes sense to me."

"No talk about it in prison, though. You told me the Rochester detectives were sure the mob didn't have the missing three million," Sarah pointed out.

"Yeah, I know. But, maybe the mob would broadcast that information."

Sarah said nothing and her silence worried me. Her mind was wrapped around something else. While we coasted slowly past the trees and bushes, I looked all over. I felt as though we were being watched. I looked for patch of white hair, but I saw nothing.

Once on the paved road, Sarah accelerated to sixty miles per hour in a few seconds. We arrived at the movie theater, on time and, somehow, in one piece. Sarah linked her arm in mine on the short walk to the theater. I looked over to her. She was looking down at the ground, her face wrinkled pensively.

"Billy, I'll tell you what's wrong with our thinking."

"What?"

"Jeb thought Gramps buried the money."

"Yeah. So?"

"Well, at least one other person must have had the same idea as Jeb."

Exasperated about her wild speculations I asked her how she knew that.

"Jeb is dead because he was looking for the three million. I'm thinking the killer is also looking for the three million."

She let me digest this idea and then continued.

"There were at least two people looking for the buried treasure. Two people who believed the mob didn't have the missing money."

I opened the door to the movie theater and she looked up at me.

"And, one was so convinced he killed the other guy."

"I think it's a bit of a stretch, Sarah."

Even though I wasn't convinced Sarah was right, I should have given her theory more consideration. But, this was our first date together and everything was shoved out of my mind except her.

The movie could have been good or it could have been bad. I really don't know. Being with Sarah, well, that was good, good, and very good. Not many forms in the seats when we entered the dark theater. I don't know if that was good or bad. Did Sarah deliberately steer us to a matinee because not many people would be there? Was she trying to keep our liaison secret? I should have asked her, but I didn't know how.

We sat near the back of the theater. About halfway through the movie I got enough courage to put my arm up around her seat. I did it casually like I needed to stretch it out. My carefully thought-out strategy was to gradually let it slip down around her shoulders, like I was just resting it there. I wasn't watching the movie as much as I was watching her, my eyes strained sideways to capture glimpses of her profile. So when I made the 'move' I didn't know it was a scary part. As soon as my arm moved down, she snuggled into me and covered her eyes. My arm immediately encircled her, hugging her tightly. We pretty much kept in the same position for the rest of the movie even though my arm fell asleep near the end. Maybe we were a bit more than friends.

When we walked out of the show, two of Sarah's friends saw us, and their foreheads wrinkled in astonishment. Oops. This won't be pretty.

CHAPTER FIFTEEN

"Hi, Sarah," said the girl with a nod to me and wink to her. Sarah ignored the suggestive wink.

"Hiya, Meg. Like the movie?"

"It was all right. Looks like you enjoyed it, though."

"Hmm. Yeah, I liked it."

No secrets in a small town, I guess. Meg, another cheerleader, was holding hands with big Jim, the tackle from the football team. He was glaring at me like he would rather take a punch than say hello. He turned to Sarah.

"How's Rick, Sarah?"

"Oh, I'm sure he's fine Jim, except for his arm."

Jim's eyes widened, the perfect season now in serious jeopardy. "What's wrong with arm?"

"It's tired from patting himself on the back so much."

The girls laughed and Jim shook his head, smiling. Not knowing what to say and, frankly, afraid to say anything at all, I remained quiet.

She said goodbye and we made our way to the car.

"You certainly are no social butterfly are you?"

I got into the car realizing my silence could be construed as me being either a dolt or stuck up. I looked out the window as Sarah drove us out of the parking lot.

"What was I supposed to say? 'Hiya, guys' like we were all good buddies?"

"Well, hello would have been good for a start. Jim's a jerk, but you knew that already. But, Meg's nice."

I looked out the window again. All my fault, huh? Yeah, right. I mean what would a cheery 'hello' have done? They might have… they might have… well, okay, they might have said 'hello' back. Well, they probably would have.

Crap! Sarah was right. I should have, at least, said hello. Now I was even angrier. It's one thing to call me out on something I did. It stings even more when the other person was right.

Sarah continued. "It's just strange for me. I go out with one guy who is Mr. Charming with everybody and you are Mr. Silent." She shook her head.

The drive to her home took about five minutes. The few times I dared to look at her, Sarah's jaw was clenched tight and her eyes were narrowed. She was pissed. Finally before we entered her driveway I spoke up.

"Sarah, look. I don't know if people here like me. It's kinda like being at a party where nobody knows you and they look at you wondering who you are and you wonder why you ever came to the party. Kinda like you don't belong."

She stopped the car in the driveway. "Billy, nobody is going to care to know you unless you at least say hello and act friendly. You hardly ever say hi to anyone in the school, either. It's like you don't want people to be friendly with you."

We stared at each other for a moment. Then I looked back out the window. She was echoing mom. And, I had to admit it. They were right. Truth was, I didn't want anyone to be friendly to me. I didn't want to be here and I didn't want to make friends. I simply wanted to have really good reasons for hating Conaroga.

My peripheral vision noted that she turned away. I looked at her profile. So pretty. And smart too, I conceded. I closed my eyes and sighed.

"I'll give it a try."

"Give what a try?" She snapped.

"You know. What you said. Say hello and stuff."

She gave me a double-take and smiled. "Jeez, you're no fun, Billy. I was expecting an argument from you. Or caveman silence."

"No argument. I think you're right."

She beamed a smile to me and got out. I stayed in the car. Sarah turned and leaned back into the driver side window.

"You, ahh, planning to come in with me?"

"Oh, yeah. Sure." I got out and just stared at the mansion.

"This bothers you, doesn't it? Big house and all."

"Oh, no. I mean..." I didn't want to be stuck up and class conscious too. But, I couldn't help it. I stopped looking at her and looked down at the ground to finish, "Well, yes. It's all so... so different."

She walked over to my side of the car and took me by the hand. "Yes, it's big, different, a mansion because Daddy makes lots of money. But, guess what?"

"What?"

"I like the cabin better." Sarah grabbed my hand and pulled me in.

Dinner was some sort of seafood dish. No fan of fish, I struggled to eat half of it. The dessert was tasty, though. Some sort of chocolate torte cake covered with a layer of real whipped cream.

After exchanging a few words with Mr. Seeley and getting one word replies, I decided to try my luck with Sarah's mom.

"Mrs. Seeley, you sure are a wonderful cook." I said rubbing my stomach.

Sarah smiled and her father raised his eyebrows as he cut into the cake. Mrs. Seeley took some time to tap the napkin to her mouth. "Oh, Billy, how sweet. Delores, our cook, does the most marvelous dishes. Though I helped a bit, the praise should be directed to her."

Mrs. Seeley smiled at me and continued to nibble away at the small helping of cake she cut for herself. I felt so stupid. I mumbled something about giving my compliments to Delores and then shut up.

After too many seconds of embarrassing silence, Mr. Seeley said, "Sarah, don't forget Rick is picking you up at seven for the youth group meeting tonight."

Sarah glared at her father who was pouring himself some coffee. She got up and reached for my hand. "I'll take Billy home. Tell Rick not to wait if I'm late."

"Oh, Bill doesn't have his own car?"

I bristled a bit, but remained silent. Sarah, however, responded with a sharp edge in her voice.

"No, Dad. He doesn't have a car. Not every kid has a high-priced lawyer for a father."

She stormed out pulling me with her. I turned toward her parents and quickly said thank-you and goodbye as I was yanked out of the room.

Sarah got into the car and slammed the door. "Sorry, Billy. He can be such a jerk at times."

She was angry enough for both of us so I tried to calm her down.

"Hey, no big deal. He didn't mean anything by it."

112

She looked at me. "Billy, he was dissing you and needling me. He adores Rick... football hero and wonderful Episcopalian."

Clearly, silence was my safest option. It's unwise to poke a hornet's nest when hornets are already swarming.

She peeled out of the driveway and I braced against the dashboard. Apparently this smiling angel had just a bit of the devil in her. After a couple seconds she had control of herself and the car, both of which I was deeply gratefully for.

"Okay. I'm done with it now." Neither of us said anything for a few seconds.

"In case you haven't noticed, my father tries to control my life. And, I don't like it."

"Yeah. I can see that."

"That he tries to control my life?"

"Well, I can see you're upset."

She gave me a fierce stare. I didn't know what to say so I changed the subject. I hadn't told her about seeing Old Tom so I decided to tell her now.

"Sarah, when we got out of the car, going to see Mrs. Patterson, I was pretty sure I saw Old Tom follow us in. Then he saw me and sped off."

She looked over to me, her blue eyes opened wide.

"Billy, maybe he and Mrs. Patterson are hunting for the treasure, too."

My face was puckered up in confusion as though she stuck a lemon in my mouth.

"Huh? Were they going out together? I mean she's married to Hank."

Sarah shrugged and her eyebrows went up. "I don't know. But why else would he be seeing her?"

"How do we know he was going to see her?"

113

"Well, obviously he was. Why else would he be turning down her driveway?"

I could think of a number of alternate explanations: he was lost and made the wrong turn, he was collecting for United Way, or maybe he had to pick up some motor oil. Or, more ominously, he might have been following us.

Then I recalled a quirk about Tom. A quirk that might actually support Sarah's intuition. "Sarah, it's always a big event for Tom when he goes to get gas for the bus. I wonder if he gets the gas where Mrs. Patterson works?"

Sarah slapped the steering with her hand. "Yes. All the buses get filled up at her gas station. It all fits. They are going out together!"

It could be true, but it was still just a guess at this point. Again. Of course, that wouldn't stop Sarah from believing it.

"Whoa, girl. She's married. Hank Patterson... dangerous criminal. Remember?"

She shook her head. "But she doesn't love him anymore. You could see that when they talked. Besides Hank Patterson is a terrible man. No, she's latched on to Tom. The only reason she would have let Hank in the home was to get information from him."

"Information?"

"Yup. Information about the money."

Sarah had a disturbing way of promoting her speculations to fact. I shook my head. How do I stop this avalanche of wild conjectures?

"You know you are jumping a bit, don't you?"

"What do mean?"

"First, I'm not one hundred percent sure it was Tom. Second, Hank is her husband. He may have just insisted upon staying with her. Or she might have offered her home with no ulterior motive; she might be what she seems to be… a nice person. Third, we don't know if Tom was deliberately going to pull into the driveway."

"So, why would he be pulling into the driveway, then?"

"I don't know. Maybe to turn around. Or maybe he was following us."

Sarah's eyes went wide.

"Of course. That's it. He could be the big shot that Hank was talking about. He knew we were searching for the treasure so he tailed us."

I shook my head. Instead of dragging Sarah away from one wild speculation, I ended up with two. Now, Sarah had Tom mysteriously following us! It was like trying to kill the mythical hydra monster. Cut off one head and two more appeared. I shook my own head a bit and I must have given her an exasperated look.

"You can't prove I'm wrong." She insisted defiantly.

"About which theory? That Tom and Mrs. Patterson are having an affair or that Tom might be involved in the robbery?"

Her eyes squeezed down to slits.

"First of all, it's wouldn't be an affair. That sounds far too sordid for Mrs. Patterson."

I rolled my eyes.

"Second, if Tom is involved with the murder, I'm sure Mrs. Patterson isn't."

I looked at her with my mouth wide open, ready to say something, but not knowing quite how to start. Finally, I closed my mouth. Before I could even think about how to respond to her, Sarah momentarily took her eyes off the road and turned to me.

"Look, Billy, we at least have to rule them out. We have to watch them. They might be the key to whole mess. Heck, Tom might have even killed Jeb."

I sighed, slumped, and stifled a scream. A fleeting glance at someone who might be Old Tom and now he's a killer. There was the sweet, incredibly nice Sarah and there was this wild person who dreamt up killer villains with imaginary motives as easily as a magician conjures tricks. She was revving up for another adventure.

"No. Stop right there. I'm not going back to her house to look through windows to check up on Maude Patterson. Hank is there and he might be a bit upset if he sees us. I don't want to see him upset in any way."

She tilted her head down and looked at me under raised eyebrows. "Duh. Of course, we won't go back to Mrs. Patterson's house."

A great sigh of relief blew out through my lips.

"No," she continued. "We'll stake Tom's house."

I sighed wearily. "I think you meant 'stake out.' We'll stake out Tom's house," I corrected.

"Good. I'm glad you agree. Mrs. Patterson gets done at the convenience store at four on Mondays; it's the one day she does the day shift. Tom is free then too. How much you wanna bet they're together tomorrow after four o'clock?"

I was exasperated. "How about a million dollars?"

She raised one eyebrow and leaned into me. "How about three million dollars?"

Sarah pulled the car into the driveway and stopped halfway near the cabin.. "Can you get Gramps' friend across the street to watch him for a while on Monday? That Mr. Singer guy?"

"Songor. Kenny Songor. Yes, probably."

"We'll do it tomorrow after school." Defeated, I got out of the car and walked toward the house. The Mustang pulled out of the drive and screeched away. I thought about Sarah for a moment. Beautiful, fun to be with, intelligent, at least in book learning, but she loved danger far too much. Oh well, I decided, you got to take the bad with the good. I hoped I would live long enough to enjoy the good.

CHAPTER SIXTEEN

Monday was my last day of suspension. Sarah met me after school at the cabin.

"How was school, Sarah? Did I miss anything?"

She looked at me with piercing eyes. The question was clever, even if I do say so myself. It could be construed as a question about school work. Or, it could be a question about how Rick responded to the knowledge that we went out the day before.

After studying me for a few seconds, she answered, "It was different."

No smile. That's all she said and I didn't dare press for anymore.

Half an hour later I was crawling through a cold, wet ditch that ran alongside Old Tom's house. Weeks ago, when I dreamed of having a relationship with Sarah, this scenario never made the final cut. I was cold, wet, and sore. And a little pissed to be cold, wet, and sore on this 'fool's errand.' I mean, really, what were the chances that Old Tom and Mrs. Patterson even knew each other? I looked over to Sarah who was happily grunting through the mud, a big smile on her face. Then I remembered something my Dad told me a few years before.

*

Dad and I were constructing a screened-in addition for our ranch house in Florida. I was grumbling about my weekend being usurped by the project and it was obvious he was frustrated as well. It was something Mom wanted and, one way or the other, she always got what she wanted. We took a break and sat on the edge of the sturdy structure where, by next weekend, screens would replace three broad openings.

"Why are we doing this, Dad?" I was hoping to tip him toward ending early so I could salvage Sunday afternoon at least. Dad looked over his shoulder at the framework we had finished. He saw things as yet invisible to me: electric wires, neat frames for tight, heavy screens, serious caulking, paint, both inside and out, and myriad nuisance tasks which pop up like mushrooms after an evening shower. With his extra vision, he had even more reason to be frustrated.

He wiped his head with a towel and looked at me with a tired smile. "It's the price of love, son."

*

Sarah looked over at me, mud covering half her face. "Almost there." She said, then giggled when she saw my face mottled with mud. I grimaced and continued slogging through the mud. Just like Dad said, "the price of love".

Finally, we stopped. Sarah and I peered over the edge the shallow gully. We were at the side of the house where the bedroom and bathroom were located.

"If they're in the bedroom," whispered Sarah, "They won't be looking out the windows." I didn't want to look in those windows if they were there.

"Let's make a run for it. Toward the bedroom window."

Those blue eyes were wide open, alert, and eager. A smile filled her face. But this time, the gully didn't get any brighter.

"Ready?" she asked. I shook my head 'no.' She looked at me sternly. "Too bad. One, two, three... let's go!"

We both scrambled over the edge of the ditch. My foot slipped and I fell down. Sarah unsuccessfully muffled a laugh. I got better footing and ran across the yard to where she was waiting by the window. She was on one side and I was on the other. Both of us were breathing hard, as much from the sprint as from just being scared.

"Ready for a peak?" Again I shook my head.

"One, two, three... peak."

She peaked over the edge of the sill, her body crouched and ready to spring away. Apparently the bedroom was empty as Sarah looked at different angles trying to see something. She ducked down again and scooted over close to me.

"Nothing. I can only see into the hallway."

Crouched down, she waddled to the corner of the house and peaked around it, her hand waving for me to follow. "Come on," she whispered. "Let's get on the porch and look in the front window." Against my better judgment we climbed the cement steps and actually tip-toed across the porch in a crouched position like two villains in a zany cartoon. Sarah crawled under the window so that she was on the other side. She held up her fingers... one, two, three. Slowly, very slowly we poked our heads up. When I first saw them at the table in the kitchen, I instinctively ducked. Sarah kept watching.

When I looked a second time, I saw Old Tom and Mrs. Patterson intently studying a map on the kitchen table. We both eased down. I looked at Sarah in wonderment. Woman's intuition? Or just a good guess? How did she figure that one out?

"They are looking for the treasure," exclaimed Sarah. "Tom is probably playing up to her to get information. Taking advantage of poor Mrs. Patterson." Sarah's eyes had narrowed, angered that her friend had been so vilely compromised. Oh, Lord, I thought, here we go again.

"Sarah..." I stopped, closed my eyes, and shook my head. She didn't jump to conclusions; she chartered planes to carry her to them.

I had to look one more time. Not at what they were doing, but how they were doing it. Tom stood with his back to me, but his arm was draped casually over Mrs. Patterson's shoulder. She leaned into him. I ducked down again. "Or planning a trip."

She raised her eyebrows and shrugged instead of saying, "Whatever."

"They looked pretty comfortable together, Sarah. Tom doesn't look like a ruthless treasure hunter. Remember he got excited about just seeing her whenever he went for gas."

Sarah thought for a moment, two fingers pressed against her lips. "You're right. She was married and he tried to keep their relationship a secret. He didn't declare his love to anyone since he was trying to preserve her respectability." Chivalry was not dead in Sarah's brain.

We snuck off the porch, ran to the ditch and sprinted back to the woods and her car. Neither of us really believed they were involved. Mrs. Patterson's marriage to Hank gave her a slight, very slight edge over anyone else as far as involvement. But Tom? Really, it was just too far-fetched. And, when I saw him following us into Mrs. Patterson's gravel drive... well, it might have just been a visit.

At the same time, I realized this was a tricky and deadly game we were playing; the prize was three million dollars. There was a pinch of possibility one or both were involved.

I was shivering by the time Sarah drove up the hill to the cabin. She wasn't shivering. In fact, she was grinning.

"Well, you know our next step."

"Next step?"

"About the robbery."

I gritted my teeth. "I didn't know there was a next step."

"Of course there is, Billy. We've ruled out Tom and Maude."

I was going to ask how we actually ruled them out, but thought better of it. Sarah continued.

"Clearly the mafia didn't get the money or else why would Jeb have threatened you and now be dead. I'm absolutely certain his death is no coincidence. Somebody else has to be looking for the money."

I didn't bother to point out to Sarah that her track record with conjectures was sullied with her self-admitted failure to implicate Mrs. Patterson and Tom. So, her use of the term 'absolutely certain' failed to impress me. What did impress me was that she was having entirely too much fun, and I was getting more and more worried.

"Sarah, that Patterson guy freaked me out. He is definitely not a nice person. And, the mob is nothing to mess with."

"Oh, come on, Billy. The mob? Really? There's no mob in Rochester anymore."

I turned away. I really didn't know if the mob was still active in Rochester, but they were alive and well in Florida. Sarah pulled in to my driveway, and I got out and walked to her side of the car. Her window was down, and she made a show of checking to make sure no one was watching. Of course, the only possible person who could see anything in our driveway was Mr. Songor and he was tending to Gramps. Her finger urged me closer so I leaned in. I tilted my head assuming she wanted to whisper something in my ear. Instead, she cupped my chin in her hand and pulled me even closer. She kissed me softly on the cheek. "Thanks for a great afternoon."

With my head still inside the window, she slowly backed the car out of the driveway. I leaned back out of the window and walked alongside. Despite being physically miserable and shivering like a surfer in a snow storm, I managed to ask the obvious. "All right, Nancy Drew, what's the next step?"

She swung into the road and yelled her answer to me.. "We talk to Anthony Rosario."

Before I could ask how, she had driven away. I sighed. She was an enigma to me. I smiled remembering her affectionate kiss less than a minute ago. As I walked back to the house, my mind wasn't where it should have been. Instead of worrying about Anthony Rosario, Hank Patterson, the mob, a dead man in Rochester, and even Old Tom and Mrs. Patterson, I was thinking of The Kiss.

CHAPTER SEVENTEEN

When I returned to school after the suspension, I was greeted with smiles and pats on the back. Everyone knew Rick had been the instigator and I had gotten a bum deal. That I took him down so easily made me a local super hero. That I also took away his girlfriend made me a celebrity. Jerry, for one, thought it was the most important event since the new Halo game came out.

"Wow! And you knocked him down." His eyes were wide, as though he just saw Big Foot or Justin Bieber.

"Not really, buddy. I just let him knock himself down. That's judo."

Tammy Washburn, a sophomore, slipped in between me and Jerry. She was one of the soccer players, a good one as a matter of fact, and cute.

"Hey, Billy. Heard you saw the new movie. How was it?"

"Oh, it was good. Pretty good."

Jerry gave her a nasty how-could-you stare which Tammy ignored. He shrugged and went down the hall which led to the junior high wing.

Once we stopped at my locker, Tammy detailed her weekend. Apparently there was some drinking party at a girl friend's house.

She was laughing. "I was slam-dunk drunk! I don't even remember the girls putting me to bed."

I looked down at her and her stare drifted from my eyes to my lips as her tongue swiped across a full upper lip. She stroked my arm. "Well, gotta get to math. Hey, call me tonight so we can talk some more, okay?"

"Yeah, I'll try to." I watched her sashay down the hall, letting out my breath slowly in a slight 'whoosh.' I closed my locker door and looked over to see Sarah leaning against the wall.

"New friend?"

My face felt hot. "No. I mean, yeah. Sorta. Seems everyone is my friend today."

"Gonna talk with your new friend tonight?" She asked as she looped her arm in mine.

We walked down the hall toward English class. "No, I never said I would actually call her. I said I'd 'try.' She nice and all, but I think I already have someone else to chat with tonight."

She smiled up at me.

"Yeah, Meg wants to talk with me about dropping Jim and maybe taking up with me."

She playfully pushed me as we walked in. Mrs. Blanchard, the English teacher, was writing some words on the whiteboard. Sarah laid her books down in the back of the classroom where she sat. "Pretty taken with yourself, huh?"

"Well, I'm a bad-ass suspended student, and I did take down Rick Henson single handedly..."

"Gosh, I'm such a lucky girl to even be talking to you."

I didn't call Tammy that evening. But, Sarah and I had a long conversation about music and movies and million dollar treasures.

*

126

The next morning Mom pestered me about taking Sarah to another movie. I protested, of course, but only for show. We both knew things were heading in that direction. In fact, I had decided to ask her face to face. But, that took some courage.

I managed to come up with five excuses to abort five opportunities during the day. Finally, after classes my courage caught up with my intentions. I didn't start face to face, however. I was looking anywhere but at her directly.

"Hey, umm... Sarah. You interested in maybe seeing that new movie, The Engagement, in the plaza? I mean, if you don't..."

"Sure. When do you want to pick me up?"

I turned to her, both eyebrows raised. It was not a question I expected.

"I... I don't have a car."

"Couldn't you drive your mom's car?"

"Well, I... umm... I don't have a driver's license."

Her head tilted down a bit, her eyebrows pierced together in a quizzical expression.

"You never got a driver's license?"

"Yes. No. I mean, yes in Florida, but I never got one for New York State."

"Why not? You've been here since June."

I bought some time by hoisting my book bag on my back and adjusting straps which needed absolutely no adjustment. "I just thought I wouldn't need one. That maybe we would be going back to Florida."

Too many times my mouth out races my mind. I regretted my words just as soon as I uttered them.

Sarah looked at me for a moment. Her blue eyes searching mine. "Because this isn't home for you, is it?"

I turned away from her stare and looked at the ground.

"You'd better get to your bus, Bill. I'll drive us to the movie." Her voice sounded flat. She walked away with no 'good-bye.' She was angry or disappointed... probably both.

I guess it's about time for me to get a license here. It didn't look like we were going back anytime soon. But, if I did get a license it kinda made staying here permanent in my mind. With Sarah as my girlfriend, I wouldn't mind staying. It really wasn't a bad place. And, Sarah was nice. Very nice. If she was my girlfriend. But is she? Sarah was going to Sunday youth groups with Rick and he was over at her house for dinner at least once last week. So Rick was still very much in the picture... and in pictures in the sports section of the local paper. Crap. Why was life so complicated?

When she called me up in the evening, both of us steered the conversation to various dramas of the day in school. There was no further discussion about me not driving.

*

The next day I was called down to Minx's office. I already had a post suspension meeting where he sermonized about the evils of fighting. Then, I simply stared at him, one word answers to his questions. I was praying this wasn't a follow-up sermon. Once in his room I sat down in my armless chair while he sat behind the desk in a cushioned swivel chair.

"Bill, you have been in school a month now. How are things going?"

"Okay."

He got up and sat on the edge of the desk, fixing his pants to straighten them out. While he attended to the crease, he asked, "Make many friends?"

"Enough."

"How's your granddad doing?"

I stared at him and answered him slowly.

128

"Fine…" I dragged out the word, like it could be a question.

"I know it's difficult watching a loved one with Alzheimer's…"

"How do you know about my grandfather?" I asked suspiciously.

"It's in your file, Billy."

He stared down at my file.

"You aren't on a sport's team. Have you joined any clubs?"

I shook my head no.

"What are you doing in your spare time?"

I shrugged.

"You're spending a great deal of time with Sarah Seeley."

The guy was starting to freak me out. How did he know that?

"Maybe you should spend less time with one person and more time making other new friends."

I was going to say, "Maybe you should stay out of my personal life." However, I figured, one suspension per week was more than enough. He got up and showed me to the door.

"Join some clubs, Taylor. Get involved. Okay." I nodded and walked out. Minx eyed me until he closed the door in my face.

I stared back at the closed door. I didn't like the guy. I didn't like that he knew so much about me. For a number of reasons, it made me nervous. Why the sudden interest in me? Why the interest in Gramps? Why the push away from Sarah? Did he know we were searching for the treasure? I closed my eyes, exasperated. Now Sarah had me thinking about a treasure! Great. I was jumping to her conclusions.

The rest of the week passed quickly. Sarah pulled me over to the junior table near the lunch line. So, I guess I was promoted from the corner table with the eighth graders. Whether it was Sarah's chiding or Minx's lecture, I was much more animated with Meg and some of Sarah's other friends, both male and female. Rick and a group of loud talking football players sat at the table beside us. Some friendly bantering went on between the two tables. Finally I was making friends.

On Friday afternoon, Sarah was beside me at my locker, leaning against the locker and making a big show of examining her nails. "Guess who I talked to last night?"

My stomach flopped again. This wasn't going to be good. "Who?"

Still focused on her hands, she answered casually. "Anthony Rosario's mom." My jaw clamped shut. I was worried about where this was going. Sarah understood my facial expression and talked quickly.

"Oh, Billy. She's such a nice lady. Hard to understand at times. Big time Italian accent. Anyway her wayward son is a mechanic at some garage in Rochester. Turns out he works on Saturday mornings."

I shook my head firmly knowing full well what she had in mind. "Oh, no, Sarah. No way. It's too dangerous."

No way were we going to Rochester to meet this guy. I said it in the car as she drove me home. I said it that night while we chatted on the phone after the game. I even said it when we drove to Rochester Saturday morning to do some shopping at the mall. Sarah wore a leather jacket covering a sheer white blouse showing a bit of cleavage, tight blue jeans, and high heels. She looked, well, very sexy. Instead of going to Marketplace Mall she took the highway into the inner city.

"Hey, where are we going?"

She laughed. "My car needs some work done on it."

"Sarah!"

CHAPTER EIGHTEEN

The large rectangular cement structure was between an old apartment building and a newer KFC franchise. An open asphalt area stretched in front of all three buildings, cars haphazardly parked here and there. Both garage bay doors were up. Inside the cavernous opening a young mechanic worked on a new Cadillac while a middle-aged man kneeled down beside a mint-condition dark blue car.

Two old men sat on lawn chairs by an ancient electric heater. A Fedora rested on one bald head and a golf cap was on the other. They wore faded flannel shirts and wrinkled black trousers, both in need of serious washing. Unlit cigars in both mouths. They watched the work solemnly, not speaking.

Inside the car, I made one final plea. "Not a good idea, Sarah. Please, let's just leave."

"Oh, you worry too much. I think Anthony is the guy fixing the blue car."

"That's a Mercedes Benz, Sarah. A very expensive Mercedes Benz."

As we exited the car, the watery eyes of the old geezers were now focused on us, or maybe just Sarah. As soon as we were between the cars the mechanics stopped and also looked at Sarah as though I was invisible. Anthony Rosario raised himself from his crouch, wiped his hands on a dirty rag and hosted a jaunty smile on a deeply lined face.

"Hi, sweetheart. What can Anthony Rosario do for you?"

Sarah smiled.

"I'm Sarah Seeley and this is Bill Taylor. We were wondering if we could chat with you a bit."

He raised his eyebrows and tilted his head down, looking over black-rimmed glasses with his great smile. It was like he was striking some pose to draw her in. "About what, little lady?"

"Kind of a private matter."

His eyebrows went up.

"Private, huh? I like that, baby. Step into my office."

The 'office' had three calendars on the walls, all turned to October, and all hosting a well-endowed female, scantily clad. A long table was strewn with receipts, business cards, papers of all sorts. The credit card device was the old kind you did manually hoping to see the receipt by pulling it hard enough across the three copies. Anthony flopped on a swivel chair in the narrow office and propped his legs up on an old packing crate. Like magic, a cigarette appeared in his mouth, already lit with him inhaling deeply.

"Whadda you want, honey?"

Sarah reached in her purse and brought out a little notebook. She looked behind her for a chair, but the only one was occupied by the former mafia man with a twirling gray cloud of smoke rising above his head and he wasn't getting up.

"We're doing a research paper for history on the Brink's robbery and we need a primary source. We were hoping you'd answer some questions."

He took the cigarette out of his mouth and sneered at her. "Shit. I can't believe this. Cops don't bother me, newspaper creeps haven't dared to come around. And you two teeny-boppers are asking me for a goddamn interview."

I closed my eyes and shook my head. Sarah would not be quiet on this one. She snapped her notebook closed. "Listen, we aren't teeny-boppers, and I don't like the trash talk. And, I'm not your honey or your sweetheart. We need this for a term paper. If you're not willing to give us an interview we'll go and talk with Hank Patterson."

Anthony's eyes widened, his feet landed on the floor, and he leaned forward toward Sarah. She hit a nerve all right. "Patterson? That asshole knows nothing. Nothing!" He looked at his cigarette. "Tell you what, sweetheart." He paused, grunted a chuckle, took a deep blast of the cigarette and blew rings toward the ceiling. "For you, I'll answer questions until this shit ciggie is done."

Sarah eyes flashed at him and put her hands on her hips. I quickly interjected to save us from either being kicked out or the latest murder victims in Rochester. "Was it part of the plan to have you beaten up during heist?"

He looked at Sarah for a moment with a smirk curling his lips and then turned to me. "Yeah. It made my part as a guard more believable. We were hoping maybe they wouldn't look so deep into my background." He took a deep drag on the cigarette. "I didn't run around with the choir boys, you know."

Oh, I did know. I shot another question at him, stopping him from another hit on the cigarette. "Who planned the heist?"

"Ahh... well, normally I wouldn't tell you, but it's okay now. It was Moreno. He was like the right hand of the Don. But, he planned something else too. He was gonna grab it all for himself."

"How do you know that?" Sarah asked.

"I know. You don't need to know how I know. I just know."

133

He watched the smoke swirl to the short ceiling. "There was a shootout in Avondale. Some cop just happened by. Moreno … he ran and left the money and one of our boys behind."

"Dom somebody?" I asked having read about the death in the article.

"Yeah. Got his head blown off."

"What was Dom's role in the robbery?"

He shrugged. "I don't know. Maybe to make sure everything ran smoothly, ya know? Did a shitty job, though. Everything went to hell."

"Were you there when he was shot?" asked Sarah.

"No. I'm tied up and blind folded in the Brinks' truck, remember?"

"Could Moreno have hid the money?"

The man looked at her, his gaze sliding from her feet all the way up to her eyes, lingering a bit too long on her breasts. She reddened. He smiled. "I'm pretty sure he doesn't have that money either."

"How do you know?" Sarah queried.

Rosario chuckled. "Sometimes Moreno was too smart."

"What do you mean?"

Anthony took a few puffs while he stared at Sarah.

"That's one of things I won't share with you."

Sarah bristled.

"Does the mafia have the money?" I asked quickly.

He looked at me over his glasses.

"Yeah, like I'm going to tell some punk kid that."

He took another drag on the shrinking stub of the cigarette.

"No. The cops got what was supposed to be for the family. You know, the bundle in the van. No one knows what happened to the other money."

"Who was supposed to get the missing money?" Sarah interjected.

"Jesus, you're a pushy bitch, ain't you?"

Sarah reddened from anger this time and I was afraid the two would come to blows in a few seconds.

Tony Rosario turned back to me and ignored her. "I would have gotten most of the money. The other two guys each would get about three hundred grand. Moreno would have gotten some too."

"After they left you, they had to have hid the money. Then, what... they drove back to Avondale? Why?" I asked.

"Beats me. Some guy Moreno knew was going to hide it outside the city, near the lake. Girlfriend's house or something. No reason to be in Avondale; that's forty or so miles south of where they should have been."

"Moreno knew where the money was going to be hidden?"

"Yeah. He knew."

"When Jeb and Hank cleaned out the armored car, did you see a guy dressed in a uniform?" I kept the questions coming faster as the cigarette got shorter.

"No, couldn't see shit with the blindfold on."

"How did they catch you?" Sarah asked.

The easy smile disappeared, replaced by an ugly sneer. "Moreno. After the shoot-out in Avondale, he 'fessed up to the Feds, then blabbed his head off."

He squashed the stub of his cigarette onto the table. Looking straight at Sarah he says: "Okay, kiddies. You are done. I gotta get back to work."

Sarah frowned. I eased her toward the door, but she pulled away.

"Look, if you remember anything else, call this number."

I watched her write her cell phone number on a page from her pad.

"Uh, Sarah…"

I tried to stop her but she yanked her arm away. She finished writing her cell phone number and handed it to the former convict. I shook my head in bewilderment. What was she thinking?

The door opened and the other mechanic slipped in the small room. The two old geezers leaned over on their chairs, looking into the room.

"Hey, everything okay, Tony?"

"Yeah." Answered Tony slowly getting up, leering at Sarah.

"Like the way you dress, honey. Let's get boyfriend out of here and have some fun."

Sarah, frozen in place, started to pale. Tony pushed me toward the door. His friend trapped my arms behind me and twisted me thru the doorway, trying to angle me out of the office. I swept his feet and he started to fall, letting go of me to brace his fall. Tony lunged at me and I moved to the side, twisting his arm so he crashed into the wall. I grabbed Sarah's arm and we lunged for the door. The younger mechanic was just rising and I kicked him in the solar plexus. He went down again, gasping for air.

We jumped over him and ran to our car. Just as I closed my car door I saw Tony, blood streaking down his face, stumble out of the garage. My window was up but I could still hear him yelling obscenities. As Sarah screeched out of the driveway, he threw a wrench at the car. It sailed harmlessly over the hood.

As we swung out into the main road, Sarah bumped the car over the curb.

I looked back for any cars following us.

"Are they following us? Anyone following us? Anyone?" Sarah screamed.

"I don't think so." I settled back on the seat and let out a gallon of pent up air.

She looked nervously in the mirror. Then she looked over to me. "Thanks." She said weakly.

I glared at her. "Jesus, Sarah."

Her face reddened. "All right. All right. Maybe I should have worn something different."

"No. That wasn't it. Or not most of it. We should have never had a chat with a psychopath."

I looked through the rear view window again to make sure we weren't being followed. We were safe. For now, anyway.

CHAPTER NINETEEN

When we got on the highway and left the Rochester skyline in the rearview mirror, I relaxed and looked at Sarah.

"We should have never gone, Sarah." I said quietly.

"Of course we should have gone," she insisted. "I just shouldn't have dressed so…"

I looked her over. "So sexy?"

She smiled and tilted her head. "You think I'm sexy in this outfit?"

I turned to her and raised my eyebrows.

She smiled. "Hmm." She turned back to the road.

Her eyes on the road, she patted my leg. "I'm sorry. Did you get hurt back there?"

"No, but fighting with the mafia is not generally a healthy pastime."

"Oh, come on, Billy. I told you, there's no mafia in Rochester. This is 2014 for heaven's sake. Rosario might have belonged to it twenty years ago, but there's no Don Corleone these days. Did you see any slick down hair in suits hanging around the garage? Or maybe you think the two guys on the chairs were some gumballs."

"That's 'gumbahs.' Sarah, did you notice the cars they were working on? The other guy was working on a Cadillac and Tony was tinkering with a Mercedes. I don't think they belonged to those two old guys."

"Billy, expensive cars don't mean mafia."

"You are so naïve."

She ignored my statement and turned onto the interstate leading us back south to Conaroga.

"You're not thinking that this Moreno guy got the money, are you?"

I thought for a moment, recalling Tony's comments.

"No. I don't think so. I mean he fessed up to the feds. Witness protection would be a 'downer' for that kind of guy. If he had the money, he would have just run far and fast."

She smiled. "Well, I'm glad you finally agree about the money being buried somewhere."

But, I didn't agree.

"The mafia has it, Sarah. Or, maybe the guy who hid it ended up on some Caribbean island drinking margaritas."

Knitted eyebrows accused me of not sufficiently embracing her theories. "No one has it, Billy. Remember Jeb thought your granddad still had it?"

"Yeah, I don't know how Jeb fits in yet."

"Oh, my God! Why can't you accept that the money is missing, buried somewhere?" Sarah said.

Fearing an argument, we both tacitly agreed to let the matter brew on the back burner of our respective brains and shifted mental gears to the upcoming matinee, a romantic comedy.

During the movie she laughed, she cried and had a good time. She left the car running when she pulled into Gramp's driveway.

"My folks are visiting some friends for dinner tonight and they want me to come too. There's a girl my age who just moved into the area. So, I can't come over for dinner tonight."

"Oh, hmm… that's all right. What about tomorrow?"

"After church. Afternoon." Her cell phone rang.

"Yes, Mom, I'm just dropping him off. I'll be home in a few minutes."

She looked at me.

"Sorry. She frets."

"I can't understand why she would ever worry about you, Sarah." I said sarcastically.

Sarah smiled and patted my hand. "Thanks for the movie. And saving me."

A pat. What does that mean? Was she still angry? Should I kiss her? I mean, she only patted my hand.

"I… uh… hey great movie. Yeah, great save. Thanks for driving. Yeah. Okay. Bye."

I walked quickly to the house, beet red with embarrassment. Will I ever know what goes on in her head?

I turned to see her using her cell phone again. She stopped the car at the end of the driveway. Probably her Mom. Or Rick. Crap. Bad thought. Just then I got a call. I smiled. She was calling me. "Hi!"

"You fu…" static interrupted the called. I held it closer to my ear. "don't mess in… out. Remember you were…" Then a dial tone. The call unnerved me; someone was trash talking on my phone.

When I looked up, Sarah was gone. I walked inside and Mom was getting dinner ready. She was too busy even to greet me. My phone rang again, and my stomach dropped. What the hell was going on? The last call freaked me out. Was Rick Henson jealous and attacking back this way? Now anger replaced fright. I clicked answer.

"What do you want?" I yelled into the phone.

There was silence on the other end for a long moment before a timid, female voice answered. "Just to talk with you a bit more." It was Sarah.

"Jeez, I'm sorry. Somebody has been calling me and then hanging up." I neglected to mention the bizarre threats.

"Not me," said Sarah. "Could be Tammy."

I laughed, worries dropping away like autumn leaves in a gentle breeze.

"Guess who I just talked to?" I could hear the smile in her voice.

"The mafia which you don't believe in?"

"Almost. Anthony Rosario. He wants to have a longer chat with us. Remembered a few more things. Things are getting interesting, Billy."

CHAPTER TWENTY

"After what happened at the garage? Sarah you could have been raped."

"No, no… he apologized and said he was way off base. Didn't want me to press charges."

"Great. We can all be good friends and have a burger together."

"How did you know?" she asked.

I shook my head, confused once again.

"Huh?"

"He wants to make it up to us by giving a few more details. We'll meet him around one tomorrow."

Butterflies rampaged through my stomach. All I could imagine was Sarah agreeing to meet Rosario in some dark alley, most of the windows boarded up with metal bars on any remaining windows.

"Where, Sarah? Where?"

"At the Dinosaur Diner. He said the burgers are on him."

I finally let the air out of tense lungs. This was a well-known restaurant downtown near the lake, famous for its large wings… 'Dinosaur Wings.' It was busy enough for us to be safe and out of the way enough that no one would recognize the daughter of Conaroga's leading attorney.

*

The next day we arrived at the restaurant after twelve. The meeting was set up for one o'clock. After a few minutes scanning the place for any of Sarah's "gumballs", we secured a table in the middle of the busy diner. People came and went while we just watched. By two o'clock we were sitting in the same seats and very much alone.

"We're being stood up!" Sarah sputtered while she searched the nearly empty large room one more time. "He never intended to meet us. He was just playing some dirty little joke on us."

Uh-oh. Red face, anger causing her eyes to fold into slits, Sarah's mood was dangerous... for both of us. She got up. "Maybe I will press charges. Let's go to the garage so I can tell him to his face."

"It's Sunday. Closed," I said, thinking that I may have just saved our lives. Walking up to an ex-mafia guy and telling him he was a jerk was like getting in an express check-out line with two bags of cement... one for each foot.

"What a bastard." Sarah said as she stormed out the door. A few moments later she was driving down an alley toward the main road. One of those dark alleys with some windows boarded up and the rest with heavy black bars. A black SUV was close enough to sniff our tailpipe but Sarah was in no mood for inconsiderate drivers.

"Back off, buddy!" she yelled hurting my ears but having no effect on the car pressing up against our rear fender. I was afraid she might stop and confront the other driver so I spoke up, trying to distract her anger. "Look, there's South Street." Just then another car drove down the alley toward us.

"Hey, this is one way." yelled Sarah. She stopped the car when the approaching Mercedes screeched up to her front fender. Men erupted from both cars. Sarah's eyes got wide. I reached for my cell phone, but couldn't pull it out my pocket.

A tall man in a short leather coat and blue jeans walked up to Sarah's door. She immediately locked the doors. I finally got my cell phone out. Who would I call? What do you do in a situation like this?

The guy outside casually looked up and down the street. Satisfied, he pulled out a gun from the back of his pants and tapped the window. Sarah unlocked the car. Finally, it dawned on me. 911. I started tapping the number, but the guy grabbed the phone from me.

"Get out, sweetheart. You too, kid. Gotta a friend who wants to see you."

When we got out, one of the men grabbed Sarah's keys and pushed past her into her seat. A moment later both of us were shoved in the back seat of the rear car. The door closed shut and the three cars wound their way through the back streets of Rochester. It all happened so fast, Sarah was speechless, which was probably a good thing.

Past abandoned apartment buildings, through a parking lot littered with glass, the convoy eventually stopped at a warehouse. The large garage door opened just as we approached it, and we drove in. After the metal door banged shut behind us it seemed like night. When our eyes adjusted, we found ourselves in a large, empty stadium-sized room. The men growled orders at us and we got out of the car. Apparently one of the leather jacket guys helped Sarah a bit too much.

"Hey, watch your hands, jerk!"

A young man with slicked-down black hair laughed and put his hands up in clear sight of everyone. "Okay, little lady, you're too tough for me." I shrugged off the arm holding me and walked beside her. I couldn't believe what was happening and part of me wanted to grab Sarah by the shoulder, shake her, and yell "See! I told you!"

Just as our eyes got accustomed to the low lighting inside the warehouse, we went through a door into the bright sunlight and were blinded again. The entourage walked quickly across an alley and then into the back door of what looked like a restaurant. I leaned in to Sarah. "No mob, huh?"

"This isn't the mob, they don't have suits on."

This got a few laughs from our escorts. The long room where we found ourselves had a single light bulb in the center and under it stood two men. In suits. Behind them an old man wearing a worn flannel shirt with gray, workman's pants, a red checkered napkin neatly tied around a thin neck. He was eating what looked like lasagna. The door near the old man was a swinging door and men in white chef suits passed back and forth in the small window. Right away I focused on the taller of the two 'suits.' He had well-groomed hair, a touch of gray, and a serious tan. He must be the leader of this bunch, maybe even the Don himself. The other guy with black hair, combed back from his forehead, had his coat jacket open. I was pretty sure he was a bodyguard or maybe a 'right hand' man. It was like we were in some painting in an art gallery, the title of which was Meeting the Mafia.

Our four escorts had stopped at the door. They remained at the door, but were watching the scene intently. There was clearly a hierarchy in this rectangular room. Sarah and I slowly walked up to the tall man who had his hands clasped behind his back. The shorter of the two 'suits' stepped toward me, blocking me from the tall man.

"You teeny boppers talked to Tony. Why?"

I don't know why I answered the way I did. It might have been my aversion to being kidnapped or that I didn't like Sarah being roughed up. Or it just might have been the 'teeny bopper' reference again. I was getting tired of hearing it. Whatever it was, I snapped out: "That's between Mr. Rosario and us."

The man stepped closer so we were nose to nose. "Look punk, who do you think you're dealing with?"

He started to push me back and my body responded automatically. A hand hold, an outstretched leg and a second later, the man was on the ground. He scrambled back up, his hand reaching inside his suit coat. A thin, raspy voice stopped him.

"Put it away, Louie."

Louie slowly took his hand from inside his coat pocket, his face screwed up in anger. He glared at me and casually straightened his coat. Then he stepped back. I looked at the tall man, but he was looking at the worker eating the lasagna. The old man in workman's clothes dabbed his mouth with the napkin, stood up, folded the napkin slowly, and put it on the table. He was short, wraith-like with his skin stretched over bones. A strong wind might have blown him over. He had a halo of white hair, but I didn't confuse him with an angel. The old man stood up and walked toward us. Louie and the tall guy stepped back. The short, white-haired man stopped right in front of me and just stared for a long moment before offering his right hand. We didn't really shake hands. He just held mine... tightly.

"I'm Robert Salvatore. You are Mr. William Taylor and Ms. Sarah Seeley." He slightly bowed to her. "Pardon the behavior of my employees. I don't hire them for their manners. Would you mind sitting down with an old man for a while?" He released my hand as though he was freeing me to make up my own mind.

His demeanor was Old World polite, and his voice was strained, weak. But behind the humility and the soft voice was raw power.

"We'd be happy to sit with you, sir." I quickly responded.

He waved us to his table, now mysteriously cleared and cleaned. Two chairs now joined his at the table.

After we sat down, he settled into his chair, and a flick of his head moved the two suits back to the far door. They were close enough to put a bullet in our heads, but far enough that we wouldn't be heard. Mr. Salvatore leaned into the candle light.

"Would you like a drink? Something to eat? The lasagna is excellent here."

I glanced at Sarah, but she just shook her head no. "We're fine, Mr. Salvatore. Thank-you."

He nodded to me and looked at Sarah. "First, Miss Seeley, my apologies for the way Tony acted yesterday. It was disrespectful and stupid. He's just a month out of jail. I have handled the problem."

I gulped when I heard this. I wondered how Mr. Salvatore may have 'handled the problem.' Beaten him to a pulp?

The little man with so much power turned to me. "William, you are brave and I respect that. But, don't be rash. A bullet from Louie can't be as easily handled as a foolish man like Tony. Capice?"

I nodded, my mouth going dry as I remembered Louie reaching into his jacket.

Don Salvatore leaned back and looked up at the ceiling; his thin fingers were framed in a steeple lightly tapping together. He looked back at me. The light conferred by one 60-watt incandescent bulb high above in the center of the room and a single candle at our table made the large room look like some sort of Neolithic cave. In the dim light I could see no color in his eyes, just black orbs outlined white, peering at me. I worried he could somehow read my mind. Frightened as I was, I didn't look away. He would certainly perceive such an action as weakness and instinctively I knew I shouldn't show any weakness to this person.

After a few seconds of silence, he began. His soft voice pulled me toward him so I could hear every word.

"You want information. I will give it to you. But, I expect something in return."

Had I been smarter, I would have stopped him right there. Instead, I just listened. "Tony didn't plan the robbery. My second in command, Al Moreno did. He let everyone think Tony was the brains behind the whole thing. To make sure there would be no... ah... difficulties during the robbery Al offered my organization a gift of three million dollars."

He shrugged and held out his hands out in front of him, palms up. "Who am I to turn down such a gift?"

He put his hands down slowly. I didn't move a single muscle.

"So about half of the money was coming to us. Money has a way of disappearing, so I sent my most trusted man with Al. This man's name was Dom."

So far, the story unfolded pretty much the way Sarah and I had pieced it together. The old man paused for a moment, looking down at the ground. I looked over his shoulder and saw the men by the door quietly talking to each other. All except Louie. He was staring right at me with his hand inside his coat ready to pull out the gun at any provocation. Mr. Salvatore looked up again and blocked the view.

"What made the robbery so good was the simplicity of the plan. Al got Tony into Brinks with false credentials. No big deal, but Al, he's careful. He pays off the guy in security who checks backgrounds. Tony, he begins working about a year before the

149

heist. Al knows this accountant... the man owed us some money. So word got back to Al about the date for a large shipment of money."

He leaned forward. "Al Moreno, he's a smart guy. Sets up the robbery perfect. But, he goes a step further. He knows how people get caught in these things. So, he had a plan about what to do with the payoff money, the three million. This money would go to the two guys who actually robbed the truck. And to Tony. Al would get a half mill. Reasonable. Al, he had good business sense."

Mr. Salvatore paused a moment, resting tired lungs. Short breaths blew out of flared nostrils.

"Al knew these dummies would spread the money all over town, in bars, restaurants, race track or wherever guys like them went. Stupid people with money do stupid things. So, Al, he decided to hide the money for a few years. Including his own cut. Less chance of tracking it."

He rested back on his chair as though leaning required too much energy.

"Al found some guy he trusted. Only Al and I knew the name. Small time operator. Not family. He gave me gifts after he... ahh... relieved people of some unnecessary burdens."

Sarah's head tilted slightly. Mr. Salvatore wasn't looking at her, but he somehow sensed it. He turned to her.

"I did nothing criminal, dear. But, who am I to refuse gifts?"

After Sarah nodded, he looked back at me. "The plan was that Al would collect the three million for us and make sure this other guy hid the rest. Only Al and Dom would know where the money was hidden."

"And the other guy as well," I pointed out.

His wrinkled face eased into a smile. "Yes, of course. Whoever hid the money would know. But here's the problem. It wasn't the old crook who hid the money. It was someone else. Someone else who Al trusted, but only he knew."

"Three million dollars, sir. How did Al know he could trust this other guy?"

"Ahh… I said Al was smart. After we found out who the guy was I have him checked out. He is forgiven a loan, a large loan and…" he looked at me intently, pausing for a moment "… and he loves his wife and son."

My stomach clenched. Dad was Grampa's only son.

"But this other someone was part of Al's plan, not mine. Let me tell you about what happened after the robbery…"

CHAPTER TWENTY-ONE

Twenty Years before, on a country road, just south of Rochester.

Al monitored the transfer of the money from the armored car to the van. After making sure the blindfold covered the face of the female guard, Jeb and Hank had ripped off their black ski masks and thrown them on the ground. Al Moreno left nothing to chance. He picked up the discarded apparel and put the two items in his coat pocket. Sloppy men, he thought.

"Pete, help these guys separate the money. Three million in this bag, three million in the other."

Pete, Hank and Jeb grabbed a bundle of hundreds for each hand and then put one bundle in the left bag and the other bundle in the right bag.

"Come on, hurry-up," said Al.

In a few minutes they were done.

Al watched Hank and Jeb carry the two large cloth bags into the van. Then they walked over to an '88 Chevy. A minute later they were gone from sight and hearing.

Al walked over and cupped his ears to the armored car, hearing a persistent scraping noise. The female guard was probably trying to cut the tight ropes against something sharp in the truck. He smiled. He'd be done by the time she was finished.

Al Moreno's blue shirt, covered a white turtle neck. New brown hiking boots completed the image of a well-to-do business man out for hike in the country. He joined Pete at the back of the van. Then he waved for another man standing on the side to join them. All three looked at the pile of money in each open bag. Al smiled and put his arm around Dominic's shoulder. "Not a bad haul, huh?"

Dom nodded. "Yeah. I ain't never seen so much in one place. Jesus H. Christ. Where's the hiding place?"

The arm still draped over his friend, Al eased him into the back seat right behind Pete who was in the driver's seat of the van. Al got into the passenger seat and then answered the question.

"Ranger Pete will take us there."

After a half hour of driving south they came to a service road leading into the park. "This is the place," Pete murmured as he stopped at a locked gate. He then jumped out and opened the gate. "Not far, now."

Two miles down the road they took a gravel path that wound up a hill. The van eased up alongside a freshly dug hole at the top. A ranger jeep was pulled up alongside. All three men emerged from the car. Pete hauled one of the heavy, canvas bags from the van and lowered it into the hole. Then he shoveled dirt on top. Al and Dom started for the van.

"Wait a minute. Let me put some pine cones and dirt here to make it look normal."

Al watched him blend the top of the hole with the rest of the surroundings.

"Just make sure the money stays in there, Pete."

"Look, I'm fine with what you did for me, Al. Whenever you guys want to dig it out, I'll let you in, don't worry. Two years from now or whenever."

"Oh, I'm not worried, Pete. We know where you, your wife, and your boy live."

Pete glared at the mobster. Then he turned around and got in the car. A moment later he was down the hill and out of sight.

Dom turned to Al. "Think we can trust him?"

"Don't worry about him, Dom. He knows the score." In a few minutes they were back on the main road.

*

"The park ranger was your granddad, William."

I looked down, shaking my head. "I know."

Mr. Salvatore spoke softly.

"Sometimes family members do things you might not like. But, they are still family. Family is important, William."

"Yes, sir."

"Dom, he was a good kid. Not smart like Al, but he was someone you could count on. Anyway Al and Dom drove back to Rochester. But, they stopped under some old railroad bridge in Avondale. No longer used and it's out of sight of the main road, so it was pretty quiet. That's where Dom was shot... and killed."

The old man looked up to the ceiling again and let out a long, slow sigh through his nose. When he looked back down his eyes glistened a bit but his voice was steady.

"Local cop happens to be nearby. Cop swings over before the van pulls out. Gun battle. Al, he escapes through the woods."

Sarah raised her hand. Don Salvatore smiled. "Yes, dear?"

"Did Dom get killed in the shootout?"

The Godfather of the Rochester family looked away into the darkness. Finally, he answered.

155

"No. The bullet which killed him was from a .45 caliber Magnum. It was the gun Al always carried with him"

"Al Moreno killed Dom?" I asked incredulously.

The old man nodded, his eyes locked with mine, as though he was looking inside my brain, for what I couldn't guess.

"What?" exclaimed Sarah. "Why would Al kill Dom?"

Reluctantly he stopped looking at me and turned toward Sarah. "The money. Al wanted all of it. Big haul. Nice retirement package."

"Oh, my God!" whispered Sarah, her hand covering her mouth as she said it.

"Al, he had no family, no connections. Smart, but no one ever got close. I always worried about him, but never thought he would kill a friend."

"So, is that what brought the cop to the bridge, a gunshot?" I asked.

"Two. Al was always very careful. He wanted to make sure Dom was dead."

"So, why didn't you… you know, take care of him."

"Like I said, Al was smart. He's being chased by the cops. Can't come back to get help from us. Not after killing Dom."

He paused for a moment, catching as much breath as he could.

"After the shootout he goes straight to the FBI and offers to testify against the family. The Feds… they lap it up. Six of my boys go to jail. Tony was one of them. Him and the other two from the robbery, I don't remember their names."

Don Salvatore sighed. "Al, he just disappears in the Witness Protection Program."

The little, old man closed his eyes and his head slumped on his chest. Dead or sleeping, I couldn't tell which. I look nervously at his men by the door, Louie the only one looking back. Then

Mr. Salvatore sighed and looked up at us, chuckling. "But Al ain't got no money and that's what he wanted in the first place. I figured he was coming back some time to get the three million."

"And you knew my granddad was the guy who buried the money."

"No, William. Not then. Al told me the small-time robber was going to hide it. I even met him. After the shoot-out. I had him brought to me. An old man. Old men are more careful than young ones, William. So, right away I figure he's okay. Anyway, he said Al never came by on the day of the robbery. He thought the robbery was off. He goes to the races in the afternoon."

Mr. Salvatore turned to Sarah and whispered. "Terrible gambler. Terrible."

He leaned back again. "Some of my people saw him there. So, I knew Al double-crossed us. Someone else hid the money, but we didn't know who. Not then, anyway."

The corners of the old man's mouth curled up, and the creases around his eyes deepened when he smiled at Sarah and me. "Tough problem, huh? We figured the money had to be south of Rochester. I had some of the boys take a van to go south and then return. Adding a few minutes to the switch over from the armored car to the van and a few more minutes to separate the money at the site, we knew the drop-off had to be within forty miles of Rochester. So we guessed about half a dozen places. Letchworth State Park was my bet."

"That was good detective work, sir." I felt stupid the second the words were out of my mouth. I mean, here I was sitting with a mafia Don in the back end of a restaurant in a less than reputable neighborhood waiting for some Al Pacino look-alike to burst in and start shooting up the place. And I praise his 'detective' work.

He looked at me and laughed. Then he coughed a bit. He drew a white handkerchief from his pocket and wiped spittle from his mouth. "Hey, Louie. William, here, thinks I'm a great detective."

Louie dropped the cigarette he was smoking and crushed it beneath one of his polished leather shoes as though it was a bug... probably one resembling me. A cold chill pushed through my body; I swallowed hard.

Mr. Salvatore turned back to us. "About a year after the robbery Al's mailbox gets a letter. We always checked his mail hoping for information we could use. Anyway, the letter said not to worry, but the money had to be moved. Nothing more. So we checked for new construction. Ruled out all the other places, except for Letchworth Park. They were building some log cabin. They used logs from some cabin two hundred years old. Made it look exactly the same. Anyway, I'm pretty sure I know where the money was, I just didn't know where it was moved to. And, I still didn't know who hid the money."

He held up a finger, which slightly trembled. "The money trail, William. It's always the key."

Mr. Salvatore stopped for a moment, looked to the side at the floor, and chuckled.

"Lots of 'money trails' in my business."

He looked back at me.

"Whoever hid the money was paid off first," he continued. "Why do I think that? Because Al stole some of the account books. He was making sure something was hid... like the identity of the guy who buried the money. Really messed us up for awhile. About five years ago, one of my accounting boys finds something in another set of records. Papers from a loan shark who died unexpectedly."

Sarah's eyes went up and once again the little man knew it.

158

Mr. Salvatore put up his hands and waved them back and forth. "No, no. Not us. This was just a heart attack. Big Sam liked fried food and ate too much of it. I warned him, but he didn't listen."

Sarah nodded to him. The bravado she had exhibited with Tony Rosario was absent; she was freaked out about this whole situation.

Don Salvatore continued.

"So, we had these papers from Big Sam. And, on one slip was the name... guess who?"

"Peter Taylor." I answered flatly.

His eyes locked with mine again, like it was just him and me talking.

"We get to your granddad's house and we find out he's... well, a bit forgetful. I can see he's got the dementia, William. He talks, but we can't make no sense of it. So we watch him to see if he gets any 'visitors.' But, just family."

The old man sighed, weary from the long explanation or maybe just weary of life.

"He's clean. We also checked you and your dad. No big money with your dad, but you know that too, don't you?"

I nodded.

"The cancer is rough on both the wallet and the heart. I'm sorry, William. Deeply sorry." He patted my hand like my grandfather used to when I was upset. He leaned back again, hands steepled in front of him.

"So why do I tell you all this? First, because you should know looking for the money is dangerous. Al is out there, somewhere. I'm sure he has come back."

He paused a moment, shallow breaths building. Then a big gulp of air and he continued.

"The other reason is this. If you find out anything about that bastard Al, you let me know. I don't care about the money. This is personal. I want Al. You see, Dom was my younger brother."

He leaned back on his chair, exhaustion obvious. The old man reached into the top pocket of his overalls, pulled out a picture, and slid it across the table toward Sarah and me. I picked it up, trying to stop my hand from shaking. A much younger and stronger looking Don Salvatore was in a suit, his arms linked with a slightly taller, stockier man with thick, black hair slicked back neatly. Both men were looking to the side at something off the picture.

"So this is why I give you all this information. You ever see the guy," he said pointing to the other man, "you tell me. Capice?"

I looked at the picture for an extra moment before setting it down. There was something vaguely familiar, but I couldn't zero in on it. I returned my gaze to the old man. He held my eyes with an intense stare.

I was sure we wouldn't pursue this mystery any further so it was unlikely I would ever meet up with Al Moreno.

"I will, sir."

He handed me a slip of paper with seven numbers on it. "If you see him, call this number, William."

He looked deep into my eyes one last time. A moment later Don Salvatore nodded slightly as though he approved of me. Thankfully he really couldn't read my mind that well because I was sure I would never be using the phone number. He winced with pain as he slowly rose to his feet. I went over to help him up. With my sudden movement, Louie brought out his gun.

Mr. Salvatore spoke loudly without even looking behind himself, "Don't worry, Louie."

Once up, he linked his arm in mine and led me toward the restaurant door.

"Now, you and Miss Seeley walk with me a few minutes. There's something I want to show you."

Wordlessly we walked with him and his entourage followed us, Louie daring to be even closer than the rest of the men. Don Salvatore shuffled through the kitchen and went through the dining area where some patrons nodded respectfully to him and others pointed excitedly. Out the front door, a few of the men who kidnapped us ran ahead and stopped traffic. The old man just kept walking as though city traffic was inconsequential.

We entered another building, a new building. Men and women were pushing carts laden with folded shirts or pants of all different cuts, sizes, and colors. It was a factory, right in the middle of downtown Rochester. Salvatore led us into an area where workers fed large machines reams of cloth. Pants were birthed out of the other end with another group of people who meticulously checked the final product. More than once we had to step out of the way of large laundry carts filled with merchandise and being pushed down the aisle.

A middle aged man, his gray-streaked hair ruffled, yelled instructions to a uniformed foreman who was leaning over the railing, a floor above us. The man turned toward us, saw Don Salvatore and waved. Shirt sleeves rolled up, tie loosened at the neck, he was obviously some sort of manager. He approached us and I could see he was a younger version of Mr. Salvatore. More hair, more flesh, more energy. He walked fast, right up to the Don and they hugged. Don Salvatore draped his arm over the shoulder of the middle aged man.

"My son, Johnny. He runs this place. This business... All American Clothes... was built with clean money, William. This year we make a profit. Not a big one. But, I'm proud of him."

161

Then I recalled the brand, All American Clothes. Too expensive for me, but apparently others were buying. I never knew they were made in Rochester.

"A regular business. Hiring. Paying our taxes. We even give back to the community too. Fundraisers, stuff like that."

The middle-aged man looked at me. "William, I think what Papa is trying to say is that this side of the family business is legit."

"Hey, I'm all legit. Whatta you telling this boy?"

"Sure, Pop. Sure."

Johnny pulled me aside, linking my arms as his father had done a few minutes before. "Pop's slowly getting the family out of the crime business. But, it takes time."

A workman walked up to Johnny and whispered something in his ear. Johnny let go of me and checked his cell phone, a look of consternation replaced the easy smile. After he closed his cell phone, he looked back at me and then his father. "Excuse me a minute." He hustled off talking to pair of workmen.

Mr. Salvatore's bony finger waved us toward a door under a bright red exit sign. A moment later we were outside in the sunlight, my eyes squinting. Sarah's car was right before us, engine running.

"Remember what we talked about, William." Then he shook my hand and walked back inside. Louie gave me a dirty look and followed the old man back into the factory. In a moment we were alone. Sarah and I quickly got into the car. After we pulled away from the curb I realized I'd been holding my breath. I let it out slowly saying, "Oh, my God!"

CHAPTER TWENTY-TWO

We never ate at the Dinosaur Diner (much to my disappointment), so Sarah took us to Jason's Diner in Henrietta. Between great, slobbering bites of the juicy burgers and fat golden French fries, we discussed what we learned from Don Salvatore.

"Do you think Al Moreno has come back?" Sarah asked.

I had just gobbled half of my remaining sandwich and all I could do was nod my head. A quick swig of Coke and I explained. "You heard Mr. Sal…" I stopped and looked around. A family of four sitting behind us and a cop a few booths down. Hmm. Probably not smart to refer to the head of the Rochester mafia.

"You heard what Mr. S said. It's always been about the money. Right now Al doesn't have any. I'm pretty sure the…" I leaned over the table and whispered to her, "… program Al was in forces people to actually work. And I'm also pretty sure Al is not too happy about any job. So, yes, Al's definitely back."

"He killed Jeb."

She was stating conjectures as conclusions again, but now I'm thinking the same thing.

"Yeah, probably. Eliminating the competition."

Sarah's face screwed up in worry. "Billy, your granddad …"

"Would be targeted," I finished, worried now, not hungry. Why hadn't I thought about the obvious connection before?

Fortunately, analytical Sarah, not wild-idea-immediately-assumed-to-be-true Sarah, quelled my fears. "If he was in the area, he'd know your granddad has something wrong with him."

I thought about it while my heartbeat pounded in my ears. A deep breath. "You're right." I conceded. "And if he asks around, folks know granddad has Alzheimer's."

"But, he might be watching, looking for clues." Mr. Songor flashed in my mind. He was around Gramps every day… listening. I hesitated, uncertain to ask the obvious, but having to… the stakes were too high.

"What about Mr. Songor?"

"Easy to check."

She got out her smart phone and googled his name. The information immediately streamed back to the screen. Leonard Songor. Born 1955. Branch manager of Rochester Savings and Trust from 1994 to 2005. Retired. A blast of air eased out of my mouth. I'd been holding my breath.

"Whew. All right, not Mr. Songor."

But, my little computer detective wasn't done. "Let's try Tom Merriweather."

"Who's that?"

She looked at me with a frown. "Old Tom." She didn't follow with a 'duh' but, the way she said his name, it wasn't necessary.

No information at all on the internet regarding Thomas Merriweather who presently lived in Conaroga. Who, Sarah said, moved to Conaroga about five years ago.

I looked at her. Sarah's eyebrows were raised into the I-told-you-so position.

"Maybe we ought to dig a little deeper into his background."

Sarah looked back at me. "You think?"

Forty minutes later we pulled into my driveway. After I got out of the car and immediately leaned both arms on the door, looking down at the ground. Mental summersaults froze me. Sarah came over, put her hands on her hips and looked at me quizzically. "What are you doing?"

"Thinking. About a whole bunch of things." I replied, straightening up. I looked at her.

"If Tom is Al, why didn't he ever contact Gramps?"

Sarah looked at me, already a few steps ahead of me in figuring out the connection. "He's your bus driver, Billy. And, he might have been talking to your granddad before you and your mom got here. Can't get much out of Gramps anymore, but his grandson who's with him day and night... "

My eyes widened as I woke up to the real possibility Tom might be Al Moreno. My bus driver and an unusually friendly bus driver... at least to me. But he didn't look like the guy in the picture that Mr. Salvatore showed us. All very confusing.

"Yeah, we definitely have to do a serious background check on Mr. Thomas Merriweather." I felt sick about once again not seeing the obvious and not taking Sarah more seriously.

Another possibility wormed its way into my brain.

"Sarah, when I was talking with Mr. Minx, he pretended he didn't know anything about me. But, he really did. And he knew about granddad being sick."

She laughed. "You think he might be Al Moreno? Oh, for heaven's sake! Just because he suspended you doesn't mean he a criminal."

"Has he been here a long time?"

Sarah scrunched her face. "No... ahh... he came a few years ago." She looked at me, eyes wide. "We'd better check him out too."

She reached for her phone and googled Michael Minx.

"Says here... let's see... hmm... graduated from Buffalo State. Ahh. Played football. Came to Conaroga four years ago. Lives at 23 Ridge Road. Looks legit."

Sarah looked down at her cell phone and started pushing some buttons.

"Did you know that Ridge Road runs parallel to the Gorge road where you live?"

She google-mapped his address. A few seconds later, a satellite map showed Minx's property. Minx was right behind Gramps' lot. "Pretty close, don't you think?" she asked.

"Yeah, too close. He used to teach in Buffalo. We could talk to people in his last school."

"Good idea."

We walked from the car to the front steps of the cabin. Sarah looped her arm in mine. Before we climbed the porch steps a car pulled up behind us and I glanced over my shoulder. It was Rick. I pulled my arm away. Sarah looked at me strangely and grabbed my arm back.

"Hi, Sarah. Bill." He said at the bottom of the stairs.

"Youth group meeting at five. We could take my car and come back and pick yours up."

"No, I'd better take mine. But, thanks for the offer, Rick." Her voice was cheery, but firm.

He nodded. "Okay. I'll meet you there."

She watched him drive off and then looked back at me.

"I gotta go. Whenever I miss one, Dad refers to it as a misdemeanor. No big deal, except for his closing statements which go on and on and on." Sarah joked.

"You could have gone with Rick to the youth group. I would have understood."

Eyebrows pierced, she looked at me. "You would have? Really?"

"Yeah. I mean, you know, if you wanted to. He's a friend, you know. Maybe your boyfriend."

Stupid, stupid statement. I regretted the words as they jumped out of my mouth, irretrievable. Why do I keep blabbing like that? Well, in this case, I know. I was pretty sure I was her boyfriend but I was worried about how much time she still spent with Rick. My heart started pounding again, hoping she would insist that I and I alone was her boyfriend. She let go of my arm.

"You think he's my boyfriend?"

No, I really didn't think so, but the wrong words slipped out of my mouth. Again.

"Well, I mean, I see you walking with him sometimes and I know he's at your house dinner sometimes."

"And that means he's my boyfriend?"

This conversation twisted from any control I may have had. Frustration slipped into anger.

"I don't know. Is he?" I demanded a bit too loudly.

She glared at me for a moment and looked away. When she fixed her stare on me again, those beautiful blue eyes were ice blue.

"Yeah. Yeah, I guess so. He's still my boyfriend. You and me, we just hang out together, huh?"

Now I was scared of losing her. I had to dial this down. So I quickly ad-libbed.

"Well, hanging out and solving a mystery, of course." I added.

She grunted. "Yeah, right. I forgot. I'm your Nancy Drew."

She curtly nodded and got back in her car. She gripped the steering wheel as though she was intent on strangling it and stared straight ahead for a few seconds. When she turned back to me, her face seemed softer.

"Billy, I..." She hesitated a moment. The bubble in my chest threatened to burst. Did I really want to hear what she was about to say?

"I... ahh... I have to get going. Bye."

"Bye, Sarah."

I walked into the house slowly. Here I had this girl who was fun to talk to, had interesting insights about people and events, and, also, she wasn't at all hard to look at. Crazy at times, to be sure, but usually fun-crazy. And, dead-on with her insights... sometimes, anyway. I really, really liked her. But, maybe she didn't feel the same way about me. I shook my head. Could she feel the same way about me? Maybe, but it's a one kiss relationship. How many kisses has Rick enjoyed? How many kisses is he still getting? Maybe I was just a convenient prop in an elaborate plan to spice up her romantic life. Or a blind idiot who couldn't tell when a girl likes him.

God, I was confused. I had to talk to her about what we were doing and where we were going. I was not going to stay in this purgatory for another day.

Boy, was I ever wrong about the last sentence. So very wrong.

CHAPTER TWENTY-THREE

The next day was awkward with Sarah. It was like we were carefully walking on thin ice, afraid to step, but having to get back to shore. We shuffled along, but cautiously and apart. What laughter we shared during chemistry and lunch was more forced than natural.

When I got back home, I let Gramps watch a nature show and I tried to call her. No answer. I hung up and didn't leave a message. Paranoia crept in the backdoor of a rattled brain. Was I right about my suspicions? Was she back with Rick? During the disastrous conversation the afternoon before so little was said and so much was left unstated. Why didn't I just tell her I wanted us to be a couple? Pushed the issue. I should have. At least that would have forced her into giving me a better understanding of where I stood with her. I resolved the next time we talked I would tell her I wanted us to be a 'couple.' End this uncertainty one way or the other.

After dinner my phone rang. I picked it up, thinking it was Sarah. It was Tammy.

"Hi Tammy." My voice was flat.

Tammy correctly interpreted my terse response as depression. "Oh, you must have heard. I'm sorry Billy."

"Sorry about what?"

"Oh, you know, Rick and Sarah."

I sat down to accommodate the sinking feeling in my stomach.

"What about Rick and Sarah?"

"Well, I saw them having dinner tonight at the Oakdale Inn. You didn't know?"

I was stunned but I wouldn't let Tammy have the satisfaction of knowing it. "Oh, no big deal. Yeah, Sarah told me. It's not as though we're a couple or anything."

"Well then how about you and me going to the dance together this Friday night. There's a party at Meg's house afterwards…"

I spent the next few minutes coming up with excuses for Friday night, Saturday afternoon late (apparently she doesn't rise very early on the weekends), and Saturday night. After we said goodbye, I laid down on the couch, arm over my eyes.

I was devastated. Gramps was agitated about something so I pulled myself up and helped him with his coins. Later he went right to bed and stayed asleep all night. I stayed awake all night feeling sorry for myself. So, I was just some pawn to be pushed along on her romantic chessboard. By morning, the dull, flatness of depression changed into spikes of anger.

Tuesday I didn't say anything to Sarah, not even a "Good Morning." Or "Hi!." Or anything at all. I couldn't. I was hurt and angry. Sarah greeted me in Chemistry class. I just nodded. She stared at me while I busied myself in jotting down notes.

When the dismissal bell sounded at 2:30, I let out a great sigh. I made it through the day without having a knock-down, drag-out confrontation with Sarah. I just wanted to get home and sleep.

By the time I got to my locker, the hallway was mostly cleared. I picked up a few books, fit them in my backpack, and then closed my locker door. Sarah was standing behind it and she didn't look pleased.

"What is your problem?" she asked bluntly.

"I don't have a problem. Not anymore."

Sarah put her hands on her hips. "What is that supposed to mean?"

I looked away from her to the floor, my nostrils flaring with blasts of air. My adrenaline was pumping in at full throttle. When next I spoke, I fumbled over the words 'you', 'ever since', and 'problem.' I took a deep breath and spewed out what was truly hurting me.

"Tammy saw you at the Oakdale last night with Rick."

"Yes. He and I were having dinner together. So?"

I bobbed my head up and down, looking more like one of those ridiculous plastic dolls than an irate boyfriend. I looked at her. My hands took over the motion from my head. "That's the problem."

"Wait a minute, buster. You said we weren't a 'couple.' So, why shouldn't I go out with Rick?"

My head was bobbing again. "Why? Why? I'll tell you why. Because he's a jerk. Your word not mine."

"Well, he wasn't a jerk last night."

"Yeah. Yeah. I'll bet he wasn't." This, of course, made no sense what so ever. I took a deep breath. The adrenaline was all spent. My anger was replaced with a terrible weight of sadness. It was over. I knew it. I looked up at her.

"Why did you go out with him, Sarah?" She studied me for a few seconds. Her breathing normalized and her expression softened. Before she looked away, I saw her eyes glisten. "You said we weren't a couple. Rick called me up and asked to go out. It was just to get a bite to eat."

"Just a 'bite to eat' at the Oakdale Inn?"

She turned back to me. "Well, that's what he said. I thought we were just going to get a burger. I had no idea we would end up there."

Then her face tightened.

"At least it was more like a real date. He picks me up in a car."

"You know I don't have a license." I whined.

"But, you could have gotten one!" Sarah snapped.

"Is that what this is about? Me not getting a license?"

She glared at me. Then her eyes softened and filled with tears.

"No," she whispered. "It's about the reason you haven't gotten a license... you aren't planning to stay here."

I didn't have a response.

She wiped her nose. "It scares me, Billy. You're not happy here. I know it. If we get involved and you leave... it just scares me."

I didn't know what to say so I went back to her first complaint, the one which didn't really mean anything. "It's not easy to get a license from out of state."

"Billy, you've been here for what, four months?"

I looked up at her. Now or never, I figured.

"Sarah, you're right about the license. And, you're right about why." She started tearing up again. I held up my finger. "Until we started going out together. After that I started liking Conaroga a whole bunch more."

She wiped her nose and had this wary look, like she wasn't sure if I was going to hit her or hug her.

"Then why didn't you care if we were a couple?" she demanded.

172

I shook my head, opened my mouth, and puffed out air. Why, indeed?

"Why? Why? Because I'm an idiot. I did care. Because I get confused when I talk to you and say stupid things. I care for you too much and I'm scared."

She didn't say anything. She just stared at me.

Well, that fell flat. I had unzipped my chest and shown her my heart and all I get was a stare. I peered at the clock on the wall. Seeing the time, I closed my eyes and shook my head.

"Missed my bus."

She looked up at the clock. "Hmm… seems you did." She sighed. We were both exhausted from the conversation.

"Well, come on, Tiger. I'll give you a lift home. Again."

Then she linked her arm in mine and we walked down the hall. Maybe not a couple, but two friends, at least, enjoying a truce.

"You're right about something, Billy."

"Me? Right about something today?"

"He is a jerk. Still. All he did at dinner was talk about himself." She squeezed my arm and looked up at me. "I don't need a fancy place to eat, Billy. And, I don't mind driving. I really don't. But, I worry about you leaving."

I looked down at the ground and nodded.

"I'm pretty sure I'm not going back to Florida, Sarah."

She looked up at me, tears filling her eyes again. "Not because you want to stay, but because you can't leave."

"Point is I'm here for the count." I said weakly.

She shook her head and, with her voice breaking, said, "Point is you still don't understand."

"I said I liked Conaroga more than a few weeks ago." I said defensively.

We walked out the door.

"And, I liked you from day one," I said, barely audible so she could ignore it if she chose

I looked back at her, curious about her response. She met my glance with a half-smile and hugged my arm a bit more tightly.

"Believe it or not, I really like to be with you more than Rick. One reason is that you, at least, listen to me. All I ever do with Rick is listen to him."

"You... hmm... you said 'one reason.' What are some other ones?" I asked grinning for the first time that day.

She gave me a sideways look. "I'd tell you but I wouldn't want your head to swell as much as Rick's."

We walked through the parking lot, hand-in-hand.

"As much as Rick's, huh? Must be a whole bunch of good reasons."

We reached her car. "Don't push your luck, dweeb without a license."

By the time we reached the cabin, our conversation was totally normal. Lord, it was good being with her. Sarah had to get back to cheerleading practice and I had to take care of granddad. I walked around to her side.

She rolled down the window. She leaned out the window and pulled my shirt so I bent down. Then she kissed me on the cheek. I caught her face in my hand and gently tilted it forward and leaned into her. This time our lips met softly.

"Hmm," she purred, "I liked that."

I leaned in for another kiss but she pushed me away.

"Easy there, Tiger. See you in school tomorrow?"

"Tonight. I'll give you a call."

She waved to me as she drove away.

I whistled as I strutted into the house. Oh, it was good on top of the roller coaster. I figured the case was more or less solved. Just some background work on Tom and Minx. I was sure Sarah wouldn't be entangling us in any more adventures. And, more importantly, I was pretty certain I now had a girlfriend. At least I was even up with Rick, star quarterback. Maybe even a bit ahead.

Unfortunately, I was correct about only one of those things.

CHAPTER TWENTY-FOUR

Mr. Songor came by after dinner. "So, how was the date, Bill?" Sarah just brought me home from school so I figured he was watching us through his window.

I tried to look serious, but my face broke into a grin. "Good."

He smiled and said, "Ahh... young love."

Mom put wide slices of homemade apple pie in front of Mr. Songor and me.

"Hey, heard on the police scanner there was a murder." Mr. Songor said between bites.

"Where? In Rochester?" I asked. Rochester seemed to have an unhealthy share of the murders in Western New York.

"No. As a matter of fact, it was in Conaroga. Over on Indian Way road."

My eyes widened. That was Sarah and Mrs. Patterson's road. It had to be Hank Patterson.

"Yeah, gunshots. Police. Some guy apparently just out of prison was killed. Might be drug-related."

More likely mob-related. I wondered how serious Mr. Salvatore was about going 'legit' with his organization. Three million dollars trumped a whole lot of good intentions. Or could Al Moreno be the murderer? I had to call Sarah. Ignoring the surprised stares of Mom and Mr. Songor, I left the rest of the pie on the table, grabbed my phone, and went into the bathroom.

After her 'hello', I launched into a quick explanation, my words stumbling over each other in a hurry to warn her.

Sarah whispered a response I could just barely understand. "I know Billy. Police cars are all over the place. One of the deputies told me it was a male, white guy. It had to be Hank. Shot dead."

"I don't know. What about Mrs. Patterson? Is she all right?"

"She found the body and called the police. Oh, it must have been horrible for her. Billy, I think we were responsible. Old Tom knew we were there."

"We gotta tell the police, Sarah."

"I know. I know. But, Billy, please don't say anything about us meeting the mafia in Rochester. My Dad will go ballistic."

In unraveling the mystery of the Brinks' robbery, we were holding many different strings, really twisted ones and we were right in the middle of an awfully tight knot. Before we could even talk the about how we might handle the police, we were simultaneously interrupted.

"Mom, I'll be right there. What? … oh, all right." Then in a whisper to me: "Billy the police are at the door, please just talk about us meeting with Mrs. Patterson, not going into the city."

There was a pounding on my bathroom door.

"Billy, get out here now!" Mom screamed in a high pitched voice.

"Same here, I think. Don't say anything about Old Tom. In case, we're wrong. Bye."

I'm not sure what prompted me to try to protect Old Tom. I guess I didn't believe the smiling man was a cold-blooded murderer. Anyway, we hung up and went to our respective mothers. Mine was none too happy.

"You didn't tell me you talked to an ex-con a few days ago." She said as she pulled me by the arm into the living room. I don't know who I was more afraid of facing: the police now or Mom later.

I breathed a sigh of relief when I saw Mr. Smith sitting on the couch. Mr. Songor was gone.

"Did you know Hank Patterson was killed last night?" No pleasantries today.

"I just found out about it. Mr. Songor told us."

"Mrs. Patterson said you talked with him last week. Tell me what you talked about." Ben wasn't giving me a chance to take a breath, let alone an opportunity to carefully consider my words.

"Well, first of all, it was me and Sarah Seeley."

"Your girlfriend?"

"Yes. I guess."

"What did you talk about?"

"It was for a term paper. We have to write one in the spring. Sarah and I thought it would be neat to do one about the Brinks' robbery twenty years back."

I told him everything about the meeting I could remember. No need to lie or stretch the truth, and with two other people giving pretty much the same story, it would be stupid to do otherwise.

After a few minutes, Mr. Smith stood up and closed his notebook. "The detectives from Rochester might have a few questions for you, but I think we're done. Billy... a bit of advice: change your term paper. Someone out there is killing people connected with the robbery. I don't want you to be collateral damage."

"I think that is a terrific idea, Mr. Smith."

Mom walked him to the door and they chatted for a while. I was nervous about what they might be discussing until I saw her

179

laughing with him. I wasn't sure where the humor could be in all of this, but I was relieved he got her into a good mood. Her hand momentarily touched his sleeve. Hmm. Divorced cop, widowed nurse. I wasn't sure I was ready for Mom dating, but I knew she was lonely and needed companionship. Dad had been gone nearly two years now. Besides, right now I needed her to be distracted, not distraught.

A few moments later Mom slowly closed the front door. I didn't know how to interpret the look on her face when she walked back. Her mind was somewhere, thinking about something. I mentally prepared myself to be slowly filleted verbally. Instead I got off with a soft warning. "I'm glad you agreed to change your topic, Billy. Steer away from this mess."

She walked into the living room, talking over her shoulder. "Mama has a date next Saturday night. You have Gramps, William."

Wow. Interesting. A bit disturbing. But right now I was just happy to have escaped the wrath of the harpy.

CHAPTER TWENTY-FIVE

I called Sarah on Sunday, but she didn't answer. She didn't show up in school on Monday either. I finally got a text on my cell phone to call. I signed out to the bathroom and finally got her to answer.

"Billy, my dad was so mad. I'm grounded for the next two weeks, and you and I can't see or talk to each other anymore."

I heard her sobbing over the phone. "I gotta go."

Click. A bit shorter conversation than I expected.

Frustration leads to anger. Disappointment accelerated the process. Walking out of the bathroom I hit the locker with my fist. I grimaced with hot pain searing my knuckles. Not a good idea to let anger make you stupid.

I walked back into study hall and flopped on my chair, looking out the window. Dark clouds were slowly moving toward us from the west. A storm was brewing. Didn't bother me much since I was already in the middle of a hurricane.

When I got back home, I fought the urge to call Sarah and almost lost the battle a number of times. Mom was oblivious to how obviously depressed I was. She just kept asking me questions about Jerry and Mr. Smith. I answered the questions as best I could, but my answers were short and my voice flat. Any other day and Mom would have pressed me on 'my attitude', but she was focused on the upcoming weekend. After Mom left for work, Gramps and I went for a walk outside.

He pulled me back into the woods always yearning for the forest he loved so much. Usually more alert during these walks, he often connected past and present. At the end of his property, there was an opening in the trees showing the neighboring house which was Minx's. The illusion of being in the park rudely ended. Gramps scowled and angrily crossed his hands back and forth. I wondered if there was something else behind his anger. Was Minx somehow involved in this mystery?

I looked down at the old man while we shuffled back along the thin deer path. I could always talk to Gramps when I was younger. Might as well try now. He might not offer advice, but he would probably be a good listener. So I blabbed and he really did listen. Sometimes, when he nodded his head, I thought he actually understood. I was holding on to his arm, making sure he didn't fall. He grabbed tightly and looked at me.

"Gonna be fine, Billy. Give it time, gonna be fine."

Was he comprehending?

"You really think so?"

"Abby, she's a gem, you know."

I closed my eyes. No, he didn't understand. And, it wasn't 'gonna be fine.' No, not all.

Instinctively, though, he held he reached over with his other hand and gently rubbed the arm holding him up. Memory gone, brain confused, he remained the gentle man I had known years ago. I looked at him again, but now his eyes were flat, not understanding anything. I hugged him. He shivered a bit in my embrace.

"Come on, Gramps. Let's get back in where it's warm."

"Okay, Johnny."

All that came out of my mouth was a mirthless chuckle. I was back to being my father, caring for his father. What a wacky life I lived.

*

The next morning I woke up to Mom slamming pots and pans in the kitchen. Rubbing my eyes, I stumbled out of bed to find out what the commotion was about.

"I can't stand that man!" She yelled seeing me standing in the doorway of the kitchen.

Oh, my God, the date was off. She had dropped from Cloud Nine and happy thoughts to ground zero, Conaroga, New York. Return of the Irate Mother.

"Mom, I'm sure he must have a good reason."

She looked at me, her eyebrows raised. "Well, you certainly take things better than I do."

"Well, it doesn't impact me as much as it does you."

"Doesn't impact you? Of course it impacts you!"

"Well, yeah, but I could have handled Saturday night. In fact, I would have liked to, Mom. Really."

She stopped slamming pots on the counter and stared at me. "Who are you talking about?"

"Mr. Smith."

"Ben? How did he get in this conversation?"

"Well, I thought the date was off."

"No. No. That blood-sucker Seeley called me up and warned me if you called Sarah up anymore he'd put a restraining order into effect."

I gulped. Could my life get any worse?

"Can he do that?"

"I don't know." She yelled, throwing the dish rag in the sink. "I'll ask someone, maybe a lawyer."

"Who?"

"Well, not Seeley, that's for sure. I'll ask Ben."

An hour later, Mr. Smith, in regular clothes, was sitting in the living room talking to Mom. I was feeling better and better about this new relationship. He turned toward me.

"So, for now, my advice would be to cool it, Bill. Don't give him reason to accuse you of stalking."

"Sarah would never testify I was stalking her."

"I'm not sure Sarah comes into this. She's a minor. I'll check with Joel Fenton, the district attorney."

Mom walked him to the door and they chatted quietly. I don't think it was entirely about Mr. Seeley.

Sarah returned to school on Tuesday but refused to talk with me. I was hoping for a phone call in or after school, but my phone just dully blinked the time. Wednesday, I noted that she had at least been staring at me now and again. Unfortunately, when I looked at her, she looked away. In the meantime, she was spending a considerable amount of time with Rick. I'm sure he had the good seal of approval from Poppa Seeley.

The last period of the day was a study hall for me on Wednesday. Mr. Sneal happened to be a proctor. At the beginning of the period, he called me up to his desk.

"Hey, Bill. Here's a pass to go to the main office. Centrifuge came in for chemistry. Go down and get it. Be careful with it, if you want to keep that A-grade."

There were other juniors he could have collared for the chore, but I liked to think he trusted me with equipment. More than once he saw me helping some of the other groups in the labs. I wound my way through the halls and soon stood in front of the superintendent's secretary. She was friendly and somehow knew me. She asked how I liked Conaroga.

"Was it a difficult transition from Florida, Billy?"

If I told her about the difficulties I wouldn't get back to study hall before the next morning.

"Difficult at first. But I'm getting used to things now."

She got up from her desk and retrieved a box from a file cabinet.

"This is what Mr. Sneal wants."

On her desk, I happened to see a roster of the bus drivers. Hmm... this might be an opportunity to get more information about Old Tom.

"Mrs. Dawson, I'm doing a biography on one of the employees for the school newspaper. On Tom Merriweather. When did he start working for the school?"

"Old Tom? What a nice man. Let's see about seven years ago. Wait, maybe six years ago. Let me check his record."

She walked to a file cabinet and I followed her. Looking over her shoulder, I might be able to pick up a tidbit or two. She thumbed through some files and couldn't find him.

"That's odd. No Merriweather, Tom."

Ah-ha!

"Oh, of course not. There it is." She smiled.

"Merwetter, Thomas. That's funny. I always remember his name as Merriweather too. Ahh... oh, here. I was right. Seven years ago."

Mrs. Dawson closed the file before I could glean any other information. The phone rang and Mrs. Dawson answered it. She grabbed a paper off her desk and went into the superintendent's office. Then I had another idea.

I opened the drawer marked P-T. Went to the end, thumbed through a few files and found mine, marked Taylor, William. I quickly picked through the papers in the folder as I listened to Mrs. Dawson talking to the superintendent in the adjoining office.

A transcript from my old school, various reports from Florida, test scores, and a sheet labeled Demographics. Mother's name, father... deceased. No brothers or sisters. Telephone number and the cabin's address. I looked at the last two pages. There was nothing in the folder about Gramps. Not as a relation, not even his name even though we were living in his house. Yet, Mr. Minx told me he knew about my grandfather from my file. Odd.

Mrs. Dawson's voice got louder; she must have been moving closer to the door. I shut the drawer just before she came out.

"Billy, you're still here?"

"Yes, just wanted to make sure I didn't have to sign for the equipment."

She chuckled. "No, no. Nothing that formal. Can I help you with anything else?"

I smiled. "No, ma'am, I have what I came for." And more, I said to myself.

I thanked Mrs. Dawson and walked back to study hall, the centrifuge heavy in my arms. So, it was Thomas Merwetter. I would check up on him later tonight, assuming the modem would kick in. Maybe even do a more detailed background check on Minx.

Unfortunately, that night a few of my friends from Florida called me up and I got distracted with them. After the lengthy phone call, the modem took too long to connect. So, Thomas Merwetter was not checked until much later. Nor was Minx. The delays proved deadly.

Sarah and I had lab together on Thursday so she couldn't avoid me then. I offered a perfunctory 'hello' and explained the lab to her. When I looked over at her, I saw tears in her eyes. If smiles could make the room brighter, those tears certainly darkened the room, the glistening points my only reference points. I felt helpless and sad. I stopped babbling about the lab and gently asked her how she was doing.

She looked at me as though I made the most stupid comment of the day. "Not good, Billy. My dad and I aren't speaking, mom talks and talks about stupid things, Rick is the one person I'm allowed to talk to and that's not fun, believe me. Not good, Billy. Not good at all."

"Well, I… ahh… I mean… I'm sorry. I… uh…"

"Billy, shut-up. I'm being a bitch now. I know it. I just can't help it."

The ruler smacked down and class started. I squeezed her hand and she squeezed back and gave a slight smile. Except for lab-related comments back and forth, we were silent.

Friday morning she actually said hello to me and gave me a smile. It wasn't exactly like the week before, but it was close. For the first time that week, she came to lunch and joked with friends who were understandably skeptical of her good cheer and cautious.

When I left the cafeteria she caught up with me and we strolled down the hall side by side. Sarah greeted her friends like she had been gone on a long trip. Right before we got to class she looked at me, a grin on her face. "I decided I could either be miserable playing by Attorney Seeley's rules or go my own way and be happy and hang out with you. Tough choice, I know… but, I've decided on the latter."

Before she went into Spanish, she leaned over to me and whispered in my ear. "Meet me at my locker after school. I think I just figured out something." Then she disappeared inside and closed the door behind her. I slowly made my way to health class. She figured something out? About us? The murders? The money? I looked at my watch. In two hours I would know.

At two thirty-one I was at her locker. Sarah dragged me around the corner, pulled me down by my shirt, wrapped her arms around my neck and gave me a full kiss on the lips. Wow. (I hope I didn't say that out loud, but she smiled so I probably did.) So, the revelation was about us.

"Billy, I was thinking. You said your granddad often said something about having tea when he played with his money."

"Yeah, with Albert Einstein. He's got dementia, Sarah."

She continued.

"In Letchworth Park there's a pull over, just one table, circular, made of stone. It's not even marked, but folks around here refer to it as the… tea table."

Right away, I figured out where she was going with this line of reasoning. Granddad hid the money. Twice apparently. The first time in the park on top of a small hill where a log cabin now resides. The second time near the tea table?

"I'm listening."

"I think he might have buried it there near the tea table." She looked around to make sure no one was listening. "It's out of the way, you have to go down a side road to get there. Overlooks the gorge. Nice spot, actually."

"Should I bring a shovel next time I go in the park?" I asked. The sarcasm made her smile and she playfully smacked me on the shoulder before answering.

"No. Well, yes, eventually, but definitely bring Gramps. The three of us are going to hunt for buried treasure this weekend."

"Uh… Sarah. You're grounded for another week. Also you aren't allowed to hang out with me. Even Mom isn't too keen on us seeing each other now. Your dad threatened us with a restraining order."

188

She flashed her eyes at me. Her eyes narrowed and I swore I could see a dark cloud form above her head. "He is such a control freak. I hate him!"

She looked out the window a few seconds. Then she sighed and looked back at me.

"Don't worry about that." She said looking at her nails, her fingers outstretched. "Dad will probably reduce my sentence. Especially if I tell him I have an important picnic on Saturday."

My eyes got wide and my jaw dropped. "You think he's gonna let you go with me?"

"Of course not."

"But, you just said that you and I were going treasure hunting this weekend."

"And Gramps. Yes."

"What? Meet you there secretly?"

Sarah closed her locker and clicked the lock shut. "Come on, Billy. How would you get there with Gramps? You can't drive. Your mother probably wouldn't drive you. No, I'll pick you up." She said this as though it was the most obvious solution. For me, however, it was altogether confusing. Very confusing.

"You're grounded, aren't you? He won't let you drive around, will he?"

"Yes, I'm grounded and no I can't drive."

Very, very confusing.

I just stared at her. "Huh?" Not eloquent, I admit, but to the point.

She started running down the hall. "Gotta catch the bus. Just be ready at ten with Gramps." Sarah disappeared around the corner. A moment later her head peaked around the edge, a big smile on her face.

"Rick will pick you up."

189

CHAPTER TWENTY-SIX

Friday night found me once again baby-sitting Gramps, listening to the football game on the radio, and wondering what concoction Sarah was brewing for tomorrow. Rick threw two touchdown passes and ran two touchdowns, one for sixty yards. He even intercepted a pass and ran for a fifth touchdown. He was formidable competition in the relationship game.

I had Gramps ready by ten o'clock and Rick drove up a few minutes later.

"Hi, Rick. Congratulations on the game last night."

A great smile filled his long face. "Thanks. Were you there?"

"No, I was listening on the radio."

"Should have been there, man. Great game."

I helped Gramps into the back seat. "I'm sure it was. Other engagements, sorry."

His eyes lit up. "Other engagements?"

"I have to watch my granddad in the evening when my mom is at work. Kinda puts a crimp in Friday nights.

"Oh," he looked in the review mirror at me and then stared at Gramps who grumbled about something. Rick backed down the driveway, stopped at the edge of the road, and waited a moment. Sarah popped out from behind some bushes and jumped into the passenger side.

"Gotta be careful who I'm seen with." She giggled.

"I'm not sure about this, Sarah," I said.

"Me either," said Rick, nervously looking up and down the Gorge Road before he pulled out.

"Oh, hush you two."

Then she leaned back over the seat and looked back at granddad.

"What do you think, Gramps? Good idea?"

He smiled, ever happy to see her, and shook his head in agreement.

"See?" she said. "He's got more sense than the two of you put together."

Rick talked about the game for a few minutes. Finally Sarah spoke up. "Rick, I saw the game last night, you told me about it on the phone this morning, and you talked about it driving up here. Change the subject."

He was quiet for a few minutes while Sarah and I talked about the changing colors of the leaves. She assured me I was in for a treat this autumn when the colors would explode like fireworks. As soon as Sarah finished, Rick started talking about the Buffalo Bills and, within a few sentences, segued to the game again. Sarah's little speech a few minutes before empowered me to reiterate Sarah's request. "Rick, buddy, I heard all about it on the radio. Don't need to rehash it."

I looked over to Sarah. "Hey, I got something for you." I reached in my pocket and pulled out a slip of paper. I handed her my driver's permit. She gave it back to me with a smile. "There's hope for you after all, Bill Taylor."

We had entered the park, but it would be a twenty minute drive to the Tea Table pull off. Rick started in about the game and simultaneously we both yelled, "Rick!" Gramps thought he had missed some sort of cue and he echoed our protest with a yell of his own. Rick didn't try talking about the game anymore.

Sarah kept looking at the trees on either side of us. Though still mostly green, they were freckled with yellow and orange. "I packed us some turkey sandwiches, and chips, and other stuff. Hope you like it, Billy."

Then her brow furrowed. "Does Gramps like turkey sandwiches? I forgot to ask."

"Sarah, Gramps eats anything."

Her face relaxed in a smile.

Granddad pointed at different places. "Over there, Johnny. Caught a poacher over there. He was killing some of the peasants." I'm hoping he really meant "pheasants."

"Commendation for that. Yup, park commissioner."

Sarah and I listened patiently to his stories, smiling at each other when he repeated himself. Even if nothing happened at the Tea Table I decided the trip was worth it. First I was with Sarah, and that was good. It would have been great had we been alone. Second, it was the most alert Granddad had been in days even if his stories weren't always coherent. I am pretty sure he didn't climb a telephone pole to save a fawn stuck at the top. Colorful memories popped out of the black brew that was his mind, all twisting reality.

It was early October and the park hosted a nearly equal number of cars, bikers, and hikers. Lucky for us, the Tea Table pull-off had no one. The entire time we were there, only one car bothered to come down the little road. It stopped at the top and turned around. Same color as Old Tom's car, but I couldn't be sure about the make. A bolt of adrenalin surged through me as I remembered that I hadn't yet checked him out on the internet.

Only after sitting down at the Tea Table for lunch did I stop worrying.

Rick ate three sandwiches, but Sarah, familiar with his appetite, had packed enough for the rest of us. I'd like to paint Rick gray with streaks of black, but that wouldn't be fair. He was nice to my grandfather, listening patiently to his convoluted stories and trying to politely untangle his words. He also was wildly enthusiastic about nearly everything. When he saw a chipmunk scurry across the stone wall his whole being was focused on the skittering ball of fur. Here was a tall, muscular quarterback, ready to be a model in some magazine, excited about seeing a chipmunk. I didn't want to like the guy, but I just couldn't help myself.

Granddad finally finished eating.

"Abby, this is mighty fine roast beef. Mighty fine. Thank-you."

It was 'mighty fine', indeed, but it was turkey, not roast beef. Rick looked at Sarah, his face carrying the questions: roast beef? Abby? She leaned into him. "He thinks I'm Bill's mother."

Soda and chewed up bits of sandwich exploded from his mouth as Rick roared with laughter. Sarah gave him an angry stare, but his laughter was contagious and we all laughed, even granddad, though he didn't know why.

While Rick strolled to the edge of the forest, trying to find the chipmunk, Sarah and I walked Gramps around the area hoping he might give us a clue about the money. No luck. Frustrated, we ceased the aimless perambulations and looked over the gorge. Down below the Genesee River had become a bright blue ribbon after the previous night's heavy rain. Sarah edged over closer to me.

"Sorry, Billy, this was the only way I could get out of the house this weekend."

I nodded.

"Good news, though. I'm no longer grounded."

I looked at her, a great smile on my face.

"Bad news is that I still can't see you anymore. My Dad thinks you're a bad influence."

"Sarah, you were the one calling the shots."

She leaned in to kiss my cheek. "I know. I know. But, Dad doesn't believe me."

"Yeah, well, you've gotta be more careful, Sarah. Even..." I stopped. Gramp's eyes were riveted on the other side of the canyon. He had been staring there for nearly a minute. I hadn't seen him this alert in years.

"Nice view isn't it, Gramps. See the river down there?"

He ignored me, his eyes intent on a region just to the left of where the gorge jutted out. He shook his finger at the location. "Johnny, look!"

"Whatta you see... Dad?"

"I can't tell you. Can't tell anyone."

Sarah and I looked at each other. My stomach flopped. I lined up my sight with my grandfather's extended arm. Layer after brown and red layer was all I saw. Except for a small black speck near the top. Everything in my mind, past memories, present thoughts, even the future with its dark paths, focused on the small black speck.

"Sarah, can I have your binoculars?"

She handed them to me and I scanned the many different layers which colored the canyon: brown, light brown, yellow, brown, red, brown, black, brown. I swung back and saw it. Barely visible from this vantage point, it looked like a small opening, dark in contrast to the strata. Probably a cave. I handed the binoculars to Sarah. She gasped.

"You can't tell anybody?" I asked Gramps.

He shook his head violently. "Dangerous."

Granddad shuffled back to the table, looking all over it. I knew what he was looking for. Reaching in my pocket, I pulled out a few coins. He immediately began separating them. His motions were jerky. He would stand up, look around toward the gorge, and sit down.

"Let's get him home; he's getting upset."

Just before I got in the car, I had that uneasy feeling of being watched again. I looked into the adjacent woods for a figure, face, or even a movement. Nothing.

"Come on, dude. Let's go." Rick urged.

I got in the car and we drove away from the Tea Table. I looked for Old Tom's car, but I didn't see it in the pull-offs.

Not wanting to excite granddad any more, we pointed out the foliage which colored the sides of the road. Soon he fell asleep in the car.

Rick pulled over at our mailbox and Gramps and I got out. I leaned back into the open window.

"I'll call you tonight." Sarah acknowledged me with a nod.

Once inside, I eased Gramps into his chair and right away he started separating coins.

I didn't see much of Mom since she was getting ready for her date. When she stepped out of her bedroom, my eyebrows went up and all I could say was "Wow!." She looked great. A few minutes later, Mr. Smith showed up clean, neat, and his teeth seemed to sparkle. They left laughing.

I called Sarah. "No date with Rick tonight?"

"Billy. Stop. There's only one guy I want to go out with."

"Hmm... who might that be?"

"Well, if it weren't for Meg, it would be Jim."

"Jerk!"

She giggled. Then more seriously she added, "That was a cave, Billy. A cave. He was staring at a cave."

"Yeah." We were both thinking the same thing: he must have moved the money there so it wouldn't be discovered when they started construction in the first hiding place.

"Billy, if we could get a rope, a long rope, we could check it out."

"No. No more, Sarah. We go to the police."

"Oh, what's the fun in that? Look, this is safe. No mob, no murderer. We're just going for a hike. Besides we can't be sure the money is there. Not unless we check it out first."

"Look, I've done some rock climbing, and it can be dangerous. That's a steep cliff."

"You did mountain climbing?"

"Dad and I did some mountain climbing before he died."

Silence on the other end. Oh, no! She was thinking. Why did I blab about the rock climbing?

"Well, then, we'll be perfectly safe. You know how to rock climb. It will be fun."

Actually, it could be fun. Watching paint dry with this girl would be fun too and a great deal more safe. "Well, you can't see me, remember?"

"Don't be stupid, I'm not going to tell Dad I'm going to see you. I'm just going to go shopping in Rochester with my friends after church. I haven't seen any of them in nearly a week."

"Sarah, I don't feel right about this."

"Oh, come on, Billy. What can happen?"

I should have listened to my instincts, of course. But an afternoon with her was just too tempting. If the climb was too dangerous, I could call it off then and we could just hike through the woods.

After some more discussion, and my reluctant agreement to her crazy scheme, we decided to meet around four o'clock tomorrow after she really did go shopping. Then, if asked, she would be able to present purchased items to daddy.

After Sarah hung up, I couldn't get her out of my mind. Teaching her some simple techniques about rock climbing would be fun. Though I would never tell her, the climb didn't look that dangerous. So, I thought about climbing with Sarah tomorrow when I should have been thinking about my unease at maybe being watched by someone. And, once again, I should have been on the internet checking out Thomas Merwetter and Mr. Minx.

CHAPTER TWENTY-SEVEN

"So, I won't be actually rock-climbing?" Sarah asked weakly.

"I don't think so. The cave is probably only about twenty or thirty feet below the ledge. I have a hundred foot rope. Pretty easy, actually. We tie it to a tree and just go hand-over-hand down. It's more like rope-climbing."

"Suppose it's more than one hundred feet?" she waited for my answer biting her lower lip.

"We don't go down, then, Sarah. You're not experienced enough."

"Could you go down by yourself?"

"Maybe. I brought my Dad's equipment, just in case."

Her gaze shifted to my boots, the rock hammer on my belt, the pitons sticking out of my jacket pocket. She seemed a bit reassured. Stopped biting her lower lip, anyway.

We were pulling into the road Jerry had led me down just a few months before. As near as I could reckon, he coincidentally showed me an area fairly close to the cave.

We continued down the bumpy path until the jostling and the overhanging branches convinced Sarah to park her car. I wondered whether granddad took this same dirt path twenty years ago.

Sarah and I got out and made our way through the undergrowth, carefully maneuvering between thorny bushes, making our way along small deer paths. I hadn't yet told Sarah about my visit to the administrative wing of the high school a few days before. "Hey, got some more information on Old Tom." I pushed a branch aside before I continued. After the branch snapped back I heard an "Ouch."

"Sorry." I pulled the branch back and led her through the narrow opening.

"I was in the main office the other day and talked to Mrs. Dawson. Found out Old Tom came here seven years ago and his given name was Thomas Merwetter, not Merriweather. That's why we couldn't find him… we were looking up the wrong name."

"What did the Internet say about the new name."

"Forgot to check it."

She reached for her cell phone. I grimaced, but stopped. I wanted to get to the cave as quick as possible. Night came quickly in the woods.

As she pecked on the screen, she filled me in on her latest find. "I finally got Dad's password for that government search site. Now we can get all the information on Old Tom."

Her finger pulled down columns of names on the screen.

"Tom Merwetter… hmm… Thomas Merwetter. Wait. Here he is."

I looked over her shoulder at the information on her iphone.

"This must be him. Retired bus driver from Syracuse… ohh!"

"What?"

Sarah looked up at me, fingers on her lips.

"His wife died of cancer."

200

Sarah's former villain morphed into the forlorn widower who found new love. I didn't think we would be doing any more snooping about Old Tom.

I suggested we also check out Minx. Sarah's expression changed from dreamy to a frown with a piercing stare. Apparently she was not too enthusiastic about being pulled from romantic thoughts about Old Tom and Maude.

"Really Billy, just because he gave you suspension doesn't mean he's a mobster!" She pushed me forward and we resumed our trek through the woods.

"I know you don't think Minx is a possibility, but I found out something about him too."

I held a branch up and she ducked under it. "What?"

"Well, he was talking to me about Gramps one day and I asked him how he knew my grandfather. He said he read it in my folder. Well, when I was at the main office, I checked my folder. No mention of Gramps. He knows too much about me, Sarah. And, besides, he kinda looks like Moreno."

"Oh, Billy, you're nuts. He looks nothing like Moreno."

"He's the same height."

She looked at me with that scrunched up face again. "Oh, yeah, that cinches it. He must be Moreno."

"Well, we should at least check."

She pulled out her phone and tapped it a few times.

"There!" she snapped and handed me her phone.

The website, govbackground.com, gave up the information on Jerry Minx. Physical Education degree from Buffalo State, teacher in Medina, New York. Not married. Actually his life was unusually detailed for the last twenty years. As though someone or some organization wanted to persuade the reader about his background. I scanned back in time. While he was in college and before, the information was sparse. I double-clicked on his year book picture. I know people change from high school, but the picture I was looking at did not at all resemble Minx now. The face was more narrow, the smile infectious, and the jawline different.

"Sarah, look at this."

She studied the picture.

"Mr. Minx?"

"Yeah, his senior picture."

She shook her head. "That's not Mr. Minx."

"I didn't think so either."

"But, Minx doesn't look like Al Moreno either."

"Plastic surgery?" I wondered out loud.

"Maybe…"

We looked at each other.

"Come on," I said. "Let's check out this cave. We have some research to do after that."

"Let's do it now," she pleaded. I reached for her hand and gently pulled her forward. She was trying to hold her phone while she was 'thumbing' on the screen. We had lost too much time and I was worried. Every now and again, the sun shined through the branches so it was like we were walking into a spotlight. A low spotlight.

"The sun sets soon, Sarah. I don't want to be climbing back up in the dark. Do you?" Sarah looked up at me with wide eyes. Then she shoved her phone back into her pocket and we continued much more quickly.

I pushed through some bushes, tripped over a small outcrop, and fell down on my hands. When I looked up, I saw I was at the edge of a cliff with the gorge opened wide for our inspection.

"Oh, this is beautiful." Sarah said as she stepped over my prostrate body. Across the gorge was Letchworth Park, miniature cars occasionally moving through a small opening in the tree-lined panorama on the top of the gorge.

I looked up and down the thin green line of grass for another, larger boulder which was just near the cave. There was a bend on the right side, so I hoped the boulder might be just out of sight. "Let's walk this way."

I walked along the edge of the cliff. Sarah held on to branches, tree limbs, bushes as the precipice was often just a foot away. For a moment she was immobilized, holding on to one particularly strong branch, looking at me like she was already on the edge of a crumbling cliff when, in fact, she was at least a yard away on a perfectly solid piece of real estate. I walked back to grab her hand and her grip was stronger than ever I remembered it.

"You know," she said with a frown, "You could at least pretend to be a bit scared."

I shrugged my shoulders nonchalantly. "Sarah, when you have hung on a cliff a hundred feet high, you don't worry about walking on top of one."

"Well, I haven't hung on cliffs too often and I'm scared, Billy."

Once we rounded the bend, I saw the outcrop ahead. "There it is. See the boulder?"

"Oh, my God. Thank you."

I didn't know if her thanks were directed at God or me or the boulder. I walked back into the woods a bit and found a sturdy pine tree about twenty feet away from the cliff. I carefully tied the rope to its trunk. I knotted it once, twice (as my father had taught me), and three times (because I had Sarah with me). Sarah watched the elaborate procedure.

"It won't slip out will it?" she asked nervously.

Tugging on the knots, I shook my head. "No, Sarah. In fact, when we leave, I'll probably cut the rope instead of trying to untangle three knots." She stayed back inspecting the knots while I tossed the rest of the rope down the cliff. As long as the cave wasn't any more than fifty feet down, we should be all right. I took a climbing harness out of the duffel bag I had been carrying. I had my Dad's helmet and gave Sarah my old one. Both fit perfectly.

"You sure you want to come down with me?"

She slowly nodded her head, but she had that deer-in-the-headlights stare. The muscles in her face worked as she clenched her teeth together.

"I'm going down with you. Tell me what to do."

Scared or not, she wasn't going to miss this opportunity for adventure.

I fit her into the harness, explaining as I guided her arms and legs. "This is top climbing and it's relatively easy and pretty safe."

I pointed to a metal device close to her stomach. "The rope goes through this belayer. If you push this red handle right here, it creates friction which will stop the rope from slipping. If you push this green one, the friction is off and you can continue going down."

"So, I control how fast I go?"

"Yes. But, I'll be at the bottom feeding you rope. So I also control your descent as well."

Mouth clenched tightly shut she started toward the edge of the cliff like she was walking the plank and about to dive into an alligator infested lagoon. She kneeled down about a yard from the edge, held on to the rope, aimed her butt toward the gorge and slowly advanced toward the edge. I stopped her and pulled her back.

"No. I'll go down first. Don't worry. Just listen to me. Okay?"

Biting her lip, Sarah's head's bobbed up and down.

"Don't slide down over the edge, you'll scrape yourself. Push off. Always keep your legs perpendicular to the face of the cliff. Watch how I do it."

I stepped on the ledge. The rope was tight as I braced myself on the edge of the cliff. I checked to make sure my belayer was switched to the green position and pushed off. Sarah gasped as I left the security of the high ground. I bounded down about ten feet below and eased myself onto a large ledge. Then, stepping to the side of the ledge, I gave myself some more slack and pushed off again. Now down about thirty feet, I put the belayer on the red and pushed out and checked out the area. No cave. Crap! Was there another boulder?

I was sweating though the waning light of the reddening sun wasn't even warm. Its rays only illuminated the upper half of the cliff. The shadowed region was slowly climbing up toward us like some dark flood water. Time was far too precious to waste right now. I pushed out again and scanned down this time. I saw it. It was about ten more feet down and farther to the right.

"What are you doing, Billy? Are you all right?"

"Just located the cave." I yelled back.

Belayer green, I descended hand-over-hand, the last few feet so I was at the same level as the cave. I accidentally looked down once and jerked my head back and stared at the rock for a moment, breathing sharply. Even though the bottom of the gorge was darker in the twilight, I could see the river, slow moving and brown, six hundred feet below. I never liked to look down when I was climbing. It was a harsh reminder of how close to death I really was. I gripped the rope more tightly.

I scrambled on the rocks toward it and reached the cave and jumped in. The opening was just a bit higher than I was tall. I attached another rope to the first rope, knotted it just once and let the rope out until it lined up with Sarah.

"You ready?" I called up, craning my neck to watch her descent.

"Yes. No. Maybe. Oh, my God. Hand over hand, right?"

"Connect the sliding loop-thing to the loop in your belt. Nothing can happen if you have that connected. The rope won't break."

"You're sure."

"Positive."

A moment later I saw her coming down slowly. She pushed off the face of the cliff and dropped down a few feet at a time. Remarkably perfect style for a beginner.

"You're doing great, Sarah. You're a natural! Just the right motion."

When she was level with the cave, I yelled for her to stop. "Push with your feet against the wall, and I'll pull you over." Sarah pushed out and I pulled the rope.

"Again!" I pulled her closer.

"Once more." She kicked off a second time and arced toward the cave but also sank down about ten feet. She landed well below the cliff and looked up at me.

"You didn't change the belayer from green to red did you?"

She looked down at her stomach, saw the green color, and slowly shook her head.

"Now what do I do?" she yelled up.

"Flip to red and start climbing up."

After a few struggling steps up, she arched her head back and looked at me with a great smile.

"So, now I'm rock climbing?"

I chuckled and said yes.

When she got level with the cave, she pushed off perpendicular to the cliff and soared through space. Feet first she landed inside, angled awkwardly back toward the opening. I pulled her arm toward me and she fell into me. She looked up at me, cradled my head in her gloved hands and kissed me full on the mouth. Not the smartest thing to do on the edge of a cliff and in an unknown cave. I pulled her in.

My heart raced from a mix of adrenaline and hormones, I held her tightly and steadied both of us for a moment. She was going in for another kiss, when I stopped her. "Easy there, tiger."

She laughed. "Oh, my God. That was so scary and so much fun. Bill, take me rock climbing sometime, please. Please!"

"It's a date."

I drove a piton into the wall of the cave and attached the rope. Then we turned on our flashlights and looked into the recesses of the cave. Once inside, it was wider than the opening. The floor extended fifteen feet to the right and fifteen feet to the left. It only went in about twenty feet before it narrowed down. Our flashlights scanned overlapping slabs of hard rock. Except for a few rocks above the smooth shale surface, there was nothing.

Sarah scowled. "Well, poop!"

"Nothing here. Nothing." I grumbled. I leaned down and shone the flashlight into some of the narrow creases. "Absolutely nothing. Damn! I thought this was it."

Nervous about the darkness climbing up the cliff. I walked back to the rope and started to unloosen it. I wanted to start our ascent as quickly as possible.

"Billy, there in that corner, not as many rocks."

I shined my flashlight and saw what she meant. The ceiling in that part of the cave slanted down so we both crouched down and waddled to the area. Not a slab of shale. Instead, it was crumbled pile of shale chips mixed with dirt. I started scooping the debris away. Shards of rock were scattered right and left as I went down about a few inches.

"I don't think it's anything, Sarah."

"Just go down a bit farther."

I sighed. My fingers had already suffered a few cuts from the sharp edges of the shale bits. I scooped up some more handfuls of dirt and pebbles.

The worn top of a handle emerged. We looked at each other in the dim light offered by the two flashlights. Sarah dropped down on her knees and we both dug furiously. I used one of the pitons to cut into the loose rock and stones. The upper part of a black suitcase was exposed. We dug around it. Then I pulled up and begrudgingly, after a rest of over twenty years, the suitcase emerged from the ground.

There, on the ground, our flashlights illuminated a black, leather suitcase, scratched here and there, with the initials PPT embossed near the broad handle. Peter Prescott Taylor, my grandfather. My heart beat wildly as I unzipped the large satchel and opened it slowly. Sarah had her flashlight pointed straight down. The white beam turned into a drab green when neatly wrapped packages of one hundred dollar bills materialized.

"We found it." I said. Sarah was right all along. A buried treasure.

In the dim light, I could see her wide eyes just staring at the contents. She hesitantly reached for one of the green bundles. It was as though she worried it was an illusion and might disappear into a wisp of green smoke when touched. She picked up the packet and counted the bills.

"How many?" I asked excitedly.

"Billy, these are hundred dollar bills. And, there are, let's see, ten, twenty, let's see… about one hundred bills in each wrap. That makes one thousand dollars in each package."

I thought a moment. "I think it's more, Sarah. $100 times 100 bills is $10,000 dollars."

She turned the packet in her hand, viewing it from all angles, holding ten thousand dollars. "Oh, my Billy, my goodness. How many bundles? How many bundles?"

I counted the rows carefully with my fingers.

"Let's see. Ahh… 18 bundles across and three bundles width wise. That makes forty-four. About four hundred thousand dollars on the top layer."

She turned to me, eyebrows scrunched together, then smiled just a bit. "Not quite right, Einstein. 18 times 3 is 54. Five hundred and forty thousand dollars in the first layer. Billy, how many layers are there?"

I pulled one bundle out, then the one below it, and counted 6 layers.

"This is it, Sarah. The missing three million."

We hugged, kissed, and hugged again laughing all the while. The kissing started to slow down and get more serious. I gently pushed her away.

"We have to get back up."

"Hmm…" Her eyes closed, she leaned in for another kiss. I compromised with a kiss on the forehead. It was a compromise with which Sarah was not happy. Nor was I, but we had to get going.

"Okay. Let's see. You climb back up the rope. Before I go up, I'll attach the suitcase to the lower part of the rope. Then I'll climb up and haul up the treasure. Good plan?"

"Yes, except for the part about me climbing up."

"Or, you can stay here and I'll…"

"I'll climb up, Billy. I'll climb. Somehow."

"Don't worry. You're a rock climber now, remember? Go slow. I'll show you how to rest on the rope."

We worked with the rope for a few minutes as I showed her how to grip her legs and hold still, giving her arms a rest. I'm not sure the lesson needed me to push her legs into various positions, but, really, I had to make sure she knew how to grip the rope. And it gave me a chance to get close to her all over again. I insisted she practice the maneuver a number of extra times, with my help, of course. Finally, she giggled and said she was ready.

Up she went and scaled the rope with as much skill and agility as an experienced rock-climber. "Sarah, girl, you are terrific!"

She yelled down when she had completed the climb. I tied the suitcase to the end of the rope... three knots. And I tied an extra rope around it to make sure it wouldn't accidentally open. Finally, I grabbed the rope, tested the suitcase one last time, and swung out. I heard a scuffing sound below me and prayed the granddad's old suitcase was rugged enough to withstand a few rubs against the sharp cliff wall. Then hand over hand, up I went. As I emerged over the edge, Sarah pulled me up. Careful not to have the container bang against the rocks too many times, I hauled it up. Once on top, I pulled the strap and dragged it a few feet from the cliff edge. The other side of the gorge was dark, entirely in shadows. The sun had dipped under the tree line. Only a red upper arc shined to us.

I untied the ropes to the suitcase. The freed suitcase was finally between us, I kissed Sarah and said, "Well, let's get this to the car."

We started to get up when we were startled by a voice from behind us.

"Yeah, but my car, not yours."

CHAPTER TWENTY-EIGHT

My stomach fell. I recognized the voice. How I could have been so stupid? All the pieces to the puzzle fell into place: where Al Moreno disappeared to; the deaths of Jeb and Hank; garbled phone calls... local number always... altered so I wouldn't recognize the voice. The clever name change. Stupid. Stupid. Stupid.

I turned around to confront the man. Less hair, more lines, the face thinner, maybe some plastic surgery too. But, the resemblance had always been there, if only my eyes had connected with my brain. It was the same face Mr. Salvatore showed me weeks before. How could I have been so blind, so long? No mistaking his identity now, especially when it's accompanied with a .45 magnum held firmly in his hand.

"Hi, Al."

He sneered. "So, you figured it out finally, huh?"

"Not soon enough."

He looked at the suitcase. "Been looking a long time for that little baby. Took me a long time to sneak out of the Witness Protection Program. Then, can you believe my luck? Your granddad forgets where he buries the money."

He grunted out a low chuckle.

"What are the odds that the man who buries the money, forgets? I mean, how can that happen? He's got dementia. So, I get a few clues, but nothing else. More and more gibberish. Then you show up. At first, I didn't like it when you started snooping around but then I thought you might be able to figure it out. Great job, Billy Boy, great job."

I ignored his sarcastic praise. I scooted away a bit away from him, closer to the ledge keeping the suitcase behind me and Sarah. "So, you killed Jeb?"

"He was a greedy bastard. Stupid too, especially the way he roughed you up."

"Worried I might have gotten hurt, Mr. Songor?" I called him by the name he had gone by for over five years. Old habits are hard to break.

Moreno grunted. "He was crude. Some things have to be handled with finesse. Trust me, the druggie was no great loss."

"What about Hank?"

"Hank? He was a loose end. He always talked too much. So I shut him up permanently."

I noticed then that Mr. Songor... well, Al Moreno... didn't talk about people as though they were people. Each victim was more like an 'it' to him. He killed Dom, Jeb, and Hank and there was absolutely no remorse. I was pretty sure I was talking to a sociopath.

"You didn't kill Tony Rosario, though."

His face darkened. "I wanted to. He was such a cocky son of a bitch. Couldn't get to him. Not a great idea for me to be in Rochester. Somebody might recognize me, even with the nose job."

Al glanced over his shoulder like he heard something in the woods. His eyes were wide. He was scared. A city boy, he was nervous in the great outdoors. It was just an animal, probably a frightened squirrel. The woods were not his element and it was getting dark. His nervousness was one of my few advantages.

"Don't worry, Mr. Songor. Deer, black bear. Both equally harmless. Just don't rile the bear." He looked over his shoulder again. Now when he talked he looked around, peering into the dark woods.

"I tried to warn you, kid."

"The phone calls. Couldn't really make much sense out them."

He shrugged.

"Did the best I could. Had to be quick and disguise the voice. But you kept at it. Guess it worked out for the best after all. I followed you to Hank's house and the park, yesterday. I was sure you were onto something."

I didn't know how to talk to a killer, especially one who might be viewing me as his next victim. So, I was quiet as we stared at each other for a few moments.

"We got a problem, you guys and me." He waved his gun at both me and Sarah.

"No. No problem. Take the money, Al. We don't want it." I scooted closer to Sarah, the suitcase now behind both of us, near the edge of the cliff.

"Oh, I got the money, kid. But, you see… you guys know too much."

His eyes had gone flat, like he had turned off his human part. The gun's barrel aimed at Sarah, slowly shifted to me, and then went back and forth as though doing some sort of silent eenie-meenie-miney-moe.

"So, what exactly happened at the shoot-out in Avondale?" I tried to keep my voice calm. I wanted to bring him back to that fateful day when he made the mistake of killing Dom with a loud gunshot. The gun stopped on me while a grim smile fixed on his face.

"Dom was a dumb ass. He did anything his brother Robert told him to do, no questions asked. When I told him we had someone new to hide the money, you know what he said?"

I kept looking at Al Moreno and I shook my head very slowly.

"He said 'sure, Al, no problem.' Jesus, he suspected nothing. I mean, come on. Wouldn't you have been suspicious?"

I shrugged, not knowing what to say.

"After burying the money in Letchworth State Park with your granddad, Dom and I drove back to the city carrying the three million. Three million for the family when nobody but me did anything. That seem fair to you?"

I shook my head no.

"I figured after I killed Dom and had the three million, I could go back to dig up the other three million. Your granddad would be whittling in front of fire by the time I got back. No one was in the park that time of year. Then a trip to St. Thomas island with six million dollars."

The barrel of the gun sagged, pointing down at the ground. Apparently holding such a large gun for a long time was difficult. Even though his arm was tired, his mouth wasn't. He seemed to enjoy talking about his past kills.

"Dom had to take a leak. He always had to piss. I already knew there was this bridge in Avondale way far away from any homes. I mean nobody ever goes there. So I had him wait until we got there. Stupid shit jumped out of the car and started pissing."

"Jesus," he chuckled, "his bladder must have been nearly bursting. I followed him, saying I got to go too. I come up behind and boom. Shot him in the head as he pissed then took a piss myself. I really did have to go. Shot him again in the back

214

when I got done. I was walking to the car when the cop pulled up. God damn it! Who would have guessed a cop would be around there?"

The gun was leveled at us again. His eyes were hooded now. Now I had to play my trump card and pray it was high enough.

"Yeah. I know what you mean. These country cops show up in the strangest places. Remember Mom's boyfriend, Ben? The police officer?"

He nodded slightly.

"He and Jerry live right over there." I pointed in the general direction of their home. "The red ranch house. You passed their house coming in."

Then his eyes narrowed. He was thinking. I hurried with my suggestion.

"Look, just let us go back down the rope. We'll get back to the cave. You take the money and go. No unnecessary noise. Not like before with Dom. Besides, you don't want to kill us, Mr. Songor." This time I deliberately used the alias he had assumed for the last three years.

He looked at the rope and followed the line back to the tree which anchored it. He smiled. "You always were a bright kid, Bill. Nice kid too. You're right. I don't want to shoot you."

Al looked at Sarah for a long, long moment before speaking again. "Okay. Good idea, Billy. Now, both of you, throw out your cell phones."

I was about to throw it into the woods when he motioned over the cliff. We both tossed the cell phones into the gorge. "Good kids. All right. One last thing before you go down to the cave. Take off your clothes, everything but your underwear. Both of you."

I looked at Sarah. "Mr. Songor, we'll freeze."

He laughed. "Once you get back to the cave, I'm sure you'll figure out how to keep warm."

"Please," I pleaded, tilting my head toward Sarah.

"Hurry up." He replied in a cold voice.

I took off my jacket, sweater, shirt, and pants, leaving on a T-shirt, underwear (thank God, I changed underwear that morning), socks and hiking boots. Sarah peeled down to her bra and panties, socks and shoes. She stared at Moreno defiantly refusing to cover up. Hooded eyes appraised her body up and down. Another time and place I would have admired her as well. But now my eyes were watching him. Looking at her he spoke to me. "Billy, throw the clothes over the edge."

I grabbed our clothes and threw them into the gorge, pants, shirts, and jackets fluttering like heavy exotic birds.

"Now, you go down first."

I thought for a moment of him alone with Sarah barely covered. I couldn't risk it.

"No, she and I go down together, Mr. Songor."

He looked back at me. "You go down first, Billy. Now!"

I kneeled down pulling Sarah back with me. "It's best we go down together so she won't fall."

His hand outstretched, his eyes lining up the barrel to point right at my forehead. "She's not worth you getting killed, Billy Boy. Just go down. She'll come right down after you. I promise."

I kept scooting backwards toward the cliff, putting the suitcase behind me so it was partially over the edge. His eyes shifted from me to the suitcase. I handed Sarah the rope, looking at Moreno while he continued to level the gun at my forehead.

"You have the money. A shot would be heard, Mr. Songor. The money goes down the cliff. Don't make any mistakes now."

Sarah was already going down the rope. I followed, watching his eyes all the while. I pushed the suitcase toward him.

Our eyes were locked. "We'll just slide down the rope and get in the cave. There's the three million."

I gripped the rope tightly and lowered myself down, out of sight of the gun and Mr. Songor. No belayers now. No helmet either. This was as dangerous as it could ever get and I hoped Sarah had the arm and leg strength to make it to the cave. She had already reached the ledge, ready for the jump off to the cave twenty feet below. I heard him pick up the suitcase when I reached the ledge. I picked up a rock in case he pointed the gun over the cliff. Wouldn't do much good, but there was nothing else I could do. I thought I heard him walking away, but I wasn't going to check.

I whispered to her that I would go down first. This way I could monitor her descent. After I went hand over hand down the rope, Sarah made no move to grab the rope. She looked over the edge at the dark drop below us. Her eyes were wide, like she had just dived in cold water and was about to scream.

"Quickly, Sarah. Hand over hand. Hold on with your legs. You can do this." I said urgently, trying to get her to listen, to focus. Panic could kill even an experienced rock climber, and Sarah was a rank beginner. Her gaze shifted from the blackness deep below to my face, still visible in the waning light. Finally she grabbed the rope and lowered herself below the ledge.

"Ouch!" Sarah's yelp alarmed me.

"What?"

"Oh, my God, a snake. Quick, keep on going Billy."

We descended rapidly twenty more feet, Sarah faster than me. Her feet were bumping into the top of my head.

"Wait, slow down, Sarah." We stopped.

"Hold tight. I'm going to kick us off toward the cave." I cocked my legs as tight as could and gave a great kick off the wall. Our arc landed us a few feet from the cave.

"Hold on tight, Sarah." I kicked off one more time. We arced right inside the cave. I stepped inside and pulled the rope in. Hand over hand Sarah lowered herself down to the entrance. "You're almost there, Sarah. You've got this. You're gonna be okay." I wasn't sure if I was trying to reassure her or myself, but she nodded and kept climbing down toward me. Then something strange happened. As I watched, everything seemed to shift into slow-motion like in the movies. One moment she was reaching her hand down toward me and the next moment she was falling and reaching up for me.

I lunged down and grabbed Sarah's outstretched hand, my wrist clasped tightly around hers. My other arm reached up for the piton, rooted in the rock. I skidded a bit. Our eyes locked, she in terror and me with an even greater fear of letting her go. She started to slip through the grip so I let go of the piton and clasped her with both hands, pulled her up. As I pulled her with both hands, I skidded toward the edge. Her sneakers found some small outcrop and she climbed up over the ledge while I yanked her in. Once on the ledge, Sarah scrambled away as though the chasm might grab her. Still on all fours, I crept toward her. When I was close enough, she collapsed into my body and started heaving large gasps of air.

She looked out of the cave. "He must have been cutting the rope as we were climbing down. Billy. He was trying to kill us!" Sarah crumpled in my arms and started sobbing. I held her tightly for a few seconds, to reassure her that I was there and to reassure myself that she was really there and hadn't fallen.

I gently stroked her blond hair, speckled now with brown dirt. "Trying and doing are two different things. We'll be safe here. He can't get us now."

We were still precariously near the edge of the cliff, but reluctant to enter the empty cave. The cold night was coming

218

fast. Sarah stopped crying, but was shivering. She looked back at the opening, it was nearly dark. "Well, we certainly can't go anywhere."

Sarah's head was on my chest. I wrapped my arms around the nearly bare, shivering body.

"We'll be all right, Sarah. People will start looking for us tomorrow. You and I will scream our heads off until someone hears us."

Warmed by each other's bodies we were momentarily fine except for our backsides which were exposed to the cool evening breeze. I pulled us far away from the edge. As much as I didn't want to let go of her, I released her and checked out different areas of the cave to find out if one place was more protected from the wind than another. It was darker, but warmer near the freshly dug hole where the money had been stored for over twenty years.

"The last time he fired a gun it brought on the police, and he lost the first half of the money. He wasn't going to risk losing the second half with a gunshot. Cutting the rope was a quieter way to get rid of us."

Sarah kept looking at her wrist. Scratching it.

"It's going to get cold tonight. If we stay close together and inside the cave we should be all right. Jerry's house is about two miles away and somebody will find your car. We'll be all right. Don't worry."

"Billy, I'm not so sure. I think something bad happened on the ledge."

Tears welled up again in her eyes and she frantically scratched her wrist.

I picked her wrist up and held it in the light that lingered in the opening. My heart sunk when I spotted two small puncture holes about an inch apart. The area around the holes was inflamed and swollen.

"Billy. The snake. It bit me. It was only a small snake but it hurt. It all happened so fast. I started down when you yelled at me. It moved so fast. I knew his head hit me and that freaked me out. But, h-he bit me, Billy. He bit me."

CHAPTER TWENTY-NINE

I examined the puncture marks in her wrist. Could it be a rattlesnake bite? Letchworth hosted a small rattlesnake population. Before the Alzheimer's robbed so many of his memories, Gramps often talked about the anti-snake bite medicine he always carried with him as a park ranger. I held the wound up to the light again. Her right arm, from her wrist to her elbow was red and warmer than the rest of her shivering body.

"It hurts, Billy. Like a fire inside my arm."

If it was a rattler, Sarah had to get to a doctor and fast. I read somewhere the bite of the smaller, younger snake was more potent than the bite of the adult. Not sure what else to do, I sat her down on the ground. She was shivering and holding her good hand to her mouth, trying to stifle an eruption of sobs. My heart was pierced with each soft cry that escaped. I gave her what I hoped was a reassuring hug and walked back to the opening. The last rays of light were kind to me; I could detect a few toe holds and some jagged rocks stuck out along the cliff face close to the mouth of the cave. Moreno was probably long gone. I had to do it. I returned to Sarah who was whimpering, hunched over, holding her wounded arm up with her other hand.

"Sarah, listen. I have to go get help."

She stopped crying, sat up, wiped her nose.

"No! No! No! How can you get back up? There's no rope."

I kneeled down, my hands gently caressing her back, trying to calm her.

"Look, I've done rock climbing without using a rope. Dad made me do it on some easy cliffs just… just in case something happened. Heck, I'm only climbing up twenty or so feet and get to the top and get help."

It was over thirty feet and the only free climbing I had ever done was in a sports store with neat little grooves and convenient outcrops with indentations to ease the climb. All Dad did was laugh when I slipped a few times before I managed to get to the top.

Sarah grabbed me with her good arm and pulled me close. I was surprised by her strength. She spoke quickly, holding me tightly. "No. I'll be all right. It doesn't hurt so much now. I'm fine. Really."

"Sarah, you have a snake bite. Probably a rattlesnake. This is serious."

The flood gates opened and she quietly cried, tears splattering the dust on the shale surface. Between sobs, she squeezed out: "I know… I'm sorry… I'm always getting you into messes… now this."

"Not your fault. But I have to get help."

"Oh, Billy, it is my fault. All of this. If I had just listened to you."

I started to get up, but she grabbed me again. Her grip with her good arm was fierce; her fingers nearly penetrated to my bone. I pried her arm from my wrist. Time was the most important factor now. I had to get help fast. "It's not your fault. Now you have to rest. Don't move around – it'll only make it worse." I took off my T-shirt and put it on her. She clenched her eyes shut as though by not seeing, it was not happening.

"Look. Keep away from the opening and try not to scratch the bite. I'll get back here with help as soon as I can."

I kissed to top of her head and she laid down in a fetal position. She was shaking as though she was having some epileptic fit. I kept stroking her, waiting for her to stop shaking so much. After a minute, she just hiccupped. Her eyes closed. Was she asleep?

I quietly stood up.

"Be careful, Billy," Whispered the huddled form at my feet.

"I'll be back for you." I said this more to reassure me than her. A moment later I was at the edge of the cave. Against the star-studded canopy of the sky, I could see a few bats hunting around the upper part of the cliff. Great. Now I have to fight bats! I looked back at Sarah. She hadn't moved and the shaking had entirely stopped.

This was going to be free climbing, the most dangerous rock climbing. I felt my heart pumping wildly. I was scared. I would have been scared if it was daytime with my rock climbing gear. This was insane. Maybe I should stay here. She might make it. I looked at her, now nearly invisible in recess of the cave. No, that was scared talk. I closed my eyes, shook my head and stepped to the edge.

Leaning out, my right hand gripping a rock inside the cave, I grabbed a small outcrop, looked for a foot groove, found it and heaved myself flat against the cliff. Oh, God! I was outside the cave, hanging on the cliff. No turning back now. I shivered in the cold and pulled myself up, my bare torso scraping against the rough cliff.

Another hand hold and I pulled myself up a few inches. My other boot barely fit into a crease between two rocks. Glancing around, I saw a small outcrop a few feet away and swung my first foot over. Just then my anchor foot slipped and I found myself hanging by my fingertips six hundred feet above the cold, hard, unforgiving ground below. I forced myself not to panic and my slow, careful probing for another foothold didn't compromise my grip. There. I found one. And there. Another one. After a few wild gasps, I kept climbing up.

A few minutes later, muscles burning, sweat making my hands slippery, I was below the ledge where Sarah had been bitten. Though I could detect the high pitched squeals of the bats, they steered clear of me. Once on the ledge the climb would be easy provided there were no more snakes on the ledge. From living in Florida I knew the cold-blooded reptiles enjoyed the residual heat of boulders and ledges. It was nearly pitch black now and I really didn't think I was going to encounter any rattlers lounging so late on the rocks. But, in the past month, luck hasn't been my friend.

I felt for another hand hold. There. Got it. I started to pull myself up when the rock slipped out of its ancient resting place, tumbling to the bottom. The foot on the same side slipped off the notch it was wedged in and I rotated away from the face of the cliff. Adrenaline surged. I didn't need it or want it. Slowly, I eased my torso back flush to the crumbling wall of rock and dirt. In the dark I felt a small root offered by a great pine tree gripping to the edge of the cliff. I grabbed it, balancing my body once more.

My heart was pounding out of my chest. Could I get a heart attack? I closed my eyes. Bad thought. Keep going up. Both feet found the smallest indentation along the nearly smooth cliff side, and I rested there for a moment, panting and trying to regain my composure. When my breathing rate steadied, I slowly crawled up those last few feet to the ledge. My right hand finally gripped the top of the warm ledge, and I pulled myself up so my arms and shoulders rested on the warm ledge. My entire body was on fire with strained muscles at breaking point. My cheek pressed against the flat surface, great heaves of air coursed through my body. It was then I heard the rattle.

CHAPTER THIRTY

The moon was still behind the trees, though a faint grayness colored the ledge so I could just barely make out the vague shape of a few large rocks. Where was the snake? The rattle again on my left. My mind stifled the instinct to jump back. I kept my hands flat, ready to heave myself up. Looking straight at where I thought the snake was, I saw blackness. I slowly tilted my head, not toward the possible origin of the sound, but away from it. Peripheral vision can better see faint stars and invisible snakes. My side vision could just make out the dim outline of the snake coiling, its rattle shaking. The snake seemed much larger than the one Sarah had described.

I freed one hand on the opposite side of the snake to feel for a rock. I found one not much bigger than an egg. Great. I'm going to kill the reptile with a stone. A deep breath... one-two-three... I hurled it at the snake and swung my leg onto the ledge and immediately stood above the reptile. It backed away a bit and coiled again primed to strike, the sound of the angry rattle my only reference point in the darkness. A moment passed, the rattle stopped, the motion started. Only when it launched itself could I easily discern its form and direction. I stepped away, almost pitching myself off the cliff. Fortunately, the motion was slow since the snake must be a bit sluggish in the cold.

The snake coiled again, its head slowly weaving back and forth. The rattling started up again.

All I knew for sure was that I couldn't be delayed anymore. But, what could I do? I shrugged my shoulders, sighed, and raised my hands way over my head, yelling as loud as I could:

"Boogie-boogie-boogie-boogie."

The snake arched away and then slithered to the other side of the ledge.

Go figure that one out.

Grabbing up, I felt for some handhold. The ancient pine again provided me a stout root. I pulled myself up and a moment later was on the plateau. Cuts and bruises covered my body, but I was safe. Grimacing with each movement, I forced my body to an upright position. The half-moon peered through the trees and gave off enough gray light to offer up the opening in the trees.

I slowly stretched my legs and then began to run. I had tricked Moreno into thinking Jerry's house was much closer when actually it was. In fact, it was about two miles away... on the road. I had about a half a mile of woods to pound through before I hit pavement, though. Piece of cake, I thought. I run two miles every day. I'll be out of the woods in a minute.

When I run, it's always with running shoes. I looked down at my feet. Clunky hiking boots. I sighed. Nothing is easy in my life. I started running, lifting the clumsy, heavy footwear and keeping a decent pace. For the first quarter mile I dodged tree limbs and ran past bushes, sharp branches and the occasional thorns scratched my uncovered body. Were it not for the heat I generated running, I was sure I would be shivering with the cold, probably pulling muscles. I thought about Sarah, alone and afraid in the cave. I picked up my speed and promptly tripped over an exposed root. Flying through the air, I tucked my right arm under my chest and rolled as I crashed into the underbrush. More scratches now but no serious injury. I resumed the run, a bit slower, a concession to fickle Mother Nature who saved me earlier with roots and now conspired to injury me with those same roots.

I ran past Sarah's car. Her keys were in her pants pocket, deep down in the gorge. Finally I emerged from the woods and ran through a field of weeds and grass. I ran faster, but it was rough terrain and I had to be careful not to sprain an ankle. At last I reached the gray, paved road. I pounded the pavement toward Jerry's house. Now my pace was faster, much faster.

I can run two miles in less than ten minutes… when fresh and with sneakers and not cut and bruised. I knew Sarah's life hung on just minutes, so I ran harder than ever before. I'm not sure whether I made it to Jerry's house in ten minutes, but I've never been so tired, so winded, or so much on fire with lactic acid. I stumbled up the porch stairs and pounded on the door.

After a few muffled yells from across the house Mr. Smith opened the door. When he saw me his eyes went wide and he helped me in. "Bill! What happened?"

My knees buckled, but he propped me up and helped me to a chair. Gasping for air I wheezed out the essentials.

"Sarah Seeley. Rattlesnake bite. Cave. Below the cliff. This side. Call 911 for ambulance."

I give Ben credit for simply accepting a serious situation. No questions, just action. Right away he was on his cell phone. "We need an ambulance out on Gorge Road. Snake bite. Sarah Seeley."

He listened for a moment. "Ahh, go to…" he looked at me for direction. Still drawing in long draught of air, I shook my head. "Look. Come to my house. The address is three Gorge Drive. We'll guide you there."

Mr. Smith repeated the message and hung up. "Should be here in about ten minutes. These guys are fast."

"There's a path to get close to the gorge." I puffed out as I exhaled. "Jerry knows where, he showed it to me." Another deep breath and exhalation. "You have any ropes? Strong ropes. We gotta get Sarah topside as soon as possible."

"Yeah. Hold on, I'll get it."

After he left I saw Jerry peering at me from the kitchen. The eight grader, for the first time ever, was speechless.

When I looked at him, he turned his head away, his face reddening. "Billy, you got no clothes on."

"Yeah, kinda of know that already, buddy. Look get me some of your dad's pants, okay?"

He ran upstairs.

"And a sweater!"

I closed my eyes and just sagged back into the chair. The breathing, at least, controlled. On the table right beside the chair was Mr. Smith's cell phone. I thought for a moment, picked up the cell phone, and closed my eyes to recall the number. Tapping the keys I got two rings before it was answered. I spoke before there was any greeting from the other end.

"Kenny Songor lives on 23 Gorge Drive in Conaroga. He's home now with a special suitcase, and he's probably packing another one for a trip. A long trip. I thought you might want to say goodbye to an old friend."

Silence on the other end of the line. Then a click.

I put the phone down. Jerry thundered down the stairs and nearly tripped over his own feet. He handed me the pants and the sweater and I got them on just as Mr. Smith came in with a long yellow rope over his shoulder and flashlight in his hand.

"Let's go." I said.

As Ben and I walked out the door, he yelled back to Jerry. "You know where this path is son, get in the ambulance and show them when they get here."

We got in Mr. Smith's car and covered the distance to the opening in less than a minute.

Ben and I jogged once again down the narrow path to the gorge. There was an understandable protest from sore muscles, but I kept a good pace. All that mattered to me was getting Sarah up. Not my screaming muscles, not the money, not the fear. Just getting her safe.

Finally we came to the opening.

"Tie the rope to that tree. I'll go down and get her."

"Billy, you're beat up, boy. I'll go down."

I shook my head. "No, Ben. Have you ever rock climbed? I have. And, I know how to get to the cave fast."

He looked at me, nodded, walked quickly to the tree, and tied the rope.

I grabbed the rope before he finished knotting it and started down the jagged rock face. I avoided the ledge. I doubted Mr. Snake had returned to his haunt, but I couldn't afford the time to play with him anymore. Hand over hand I went down quickly to the correct distance, pushed off the cliff face, arced out into the black emptiness. Wham! I hit the wall beside the cave opening. I slammed into the rocks so violently I almost let go. So much for my rock climbing experience and knowing where the cave was. At least it was too dark for Ben to see my blunder. After bouncing back to my starting point, I pushed off again more carefully and landed in the cave. I then felt the side of the opening for the piton and tied the rope to it.

Sarah was huddled in the same place. She was shivering so I thought she would be cold. When I felt her arm, though, he was hot to the touch.

"Sarah. Wake up. It's me, Billy."

"Ohh. Billy. My head." Her voice was slurred like she was about to fall asleep. Man, we were cutting it close.

I gently tried to pull her under her arm pits. She had sweat so much she almost slipped from my grasp.

"Ouch my arm."

"Sorry. Listen, can you walk?"

As I supported her, she took a few steps. "Hurts, Billy."

We made our way to the opening, me propping her up. "Where does it hurt?"

"All over my arm. All over."

"Help is coming. We gotta get you up outta here."

She held up her bad arm, trying not to move it and wincing with pain when she did. The other arm she wrapped around my neck. I grabbed the rope and wrapped it around us, knotting it to hold us together.

She kissed my neck.

"You came back," She mumbled.

"Just stay awake, Sarah. You've got to hold on tight to my neck." Her head nodded rubbing against my chest. I slapped one of her cheeks, trying to keep her focus on me. Startled awake, she shook her head.

"I will, Billy. I'll tryyyy."

"Pull us up, Ben." I yelled.

The rope went up a foot at a time. I did the best I could to find outcrops to place my foot on and push us up more, but it was difficult. About half way up, Sarah's bad arm flopped down and good hand relaxed. She started to slide through my grasp. I held her even tighter, muscles red hot with pain, but wet as she was, she continued slipping through my grasp.

"Sarah! Sarah! Wake-up."

"Oh, shorry. Tired. Sho tired."

"Hold my neck, Sarah. Hold tight." Another foot up. Sarah slipped another inch down.

"Oh, Billy. Hurt. Sleep."

I tilted my head down and bit her shoulder, I think I might have drawn blood. Her head snapped up, angry, alert.

"Hey!" She yelled. "What are you doing?"

"Hold on to me, Sarah. Hold tight."

She grasped my neck again, muttered in protest and clung tightly to me. Another foot up. She was no longer slipping.

Finally we reached the top. Outstretched arms eased an unconscious Sarah from my grasp. It couldn't have been Ben's arms, however, because the rope continued its steady one foot up-pause-one foot up motion, scratching my stomach on a rock. When I lifted myself up over the edge, I looked up and saw Rick Henson carrying Sarah away down the path, her head resting on his shoulder and her unclad body tastefully covered by a blanket.

CHAPTER THIRTY-ONE

In Greek mythology there are three blind, old hags who weave the fabric of our lives. They were called the Fates. I am sure they must have enjoyed a few giggles over the knots they tied in my worn cloth.

What star quarterback happened to be volunteering for ambulance service Sunday evening? Good guess! Rick Henson. On that particular day a newspaper reporter from the Rochester paper just happened to respond to the ambulance call. He followed the ambulance to the opening and, just as he got his camera out of its bag, into the beam of the headlights comes Rick carrying Sarah. A perfect picture, naturally. Of course, it made the front page. The front page of the local paper and most of the newspapers in Western New York. Also the internet. Football star, National Honor Society, and volunteer paramedic were all mentioned in the article. Oh, the heading for the story? "Football Star Saves Girlfriend." By the time I limped out of the woods, the ambulance was a twirling red light racing toward the hospital in Rochester. Yeah, those old hags were definitely laughing at me.

Two paramedics fussed over me, but I wanted to follow the ambulance carrying Sarah so I brushed them off. I was going to hitch a ride with Mr. Smith when I saw Mom, heavy wool sweater on, hugging her arms. In a few moments those arms were around me. Gramps ambled out of the car, confused. When he saw us he joined the hug. Despite the pain, fatigue, and maybe losing Sarah to Rick Henson again, it felt pretty good.

Mom drove me to Rochester and insisted I get some medical attention. After an hour wait, a doctor cleaned my wounds and I had an IV filling me with fluids. In another hour I was deemed fit and released. I found out where Sarah's room was and tapped on the door. No one answered so I slowly swung the door open. I stopped in the doorway. Mr. And Mrs. Seeley were a few feet from the bed. Sitting on a chair beside her was none other than Rick Henson, holding her hand and talking to her. I was debating about going in or just leaving when Mr. Seeley saw me. He pushed me out into the hall and hissed at me.

"You! Get out of here. Haven't you done enough damage? Just leave, Taylor, and don't ever see my daughter again. And tell your mother I was serious about that restraining order!"

Well, that sort of made up my mind. Red faced, I walked to the car where Mom and Gramps were waiting.

"How was Sarah?"

I closed the door and looked out the window. "Doing fine, Mom. Doing just fine. Let's go home… please."

*

The next day Mom wanted me to stay home from school. Good idea. Every muscle, I mean every single muscle from my hamstrings to the ones in my fingers even some of my scalp muscles, protested even the most minimal movement. Nevertheless, I was determined to go to school. It was that or mope around the cabin all day. Not wanting to give Mom a reason for pushing the matter, I was all smiles and talk. But when she looked away or checked on Gramps, I nearly collapsed.

I said goodbye while she fed Gramps. When I walked toward the front door, gritting my teeth to hide the pain, she yelled to me.

"Don't think I'm bamboozled by your act, Billy. I know you're hurting. You should stay home, but you're as stubborn as your father. Just go slow today."

I stopped, turned my head. "Okay, I'll go slow, Mom." What else could I say?

My face had no scratches on it, so with my long-sleeved shirt no one would ever see my cuts and bruises.

At school I saw the morning paper. I mean, I couldn't miss it. At least a hundred kids carried the newspaper with their books that day. Probably the first time most of them had ever read a newspaper other than the sports section. The article talked all about Rick. There was no mention of me.

"Missed a great chance, Bill."

"She finally came to her senses, asshole."

"What a loser."

"Billy, if you want to go to the dance…"

I felt like throwing up. Sarah wasn't in school, but that wasn't surprising. Rick hadn't returned either and that was disconcerting. My guess was that he was a great comfort to her in the hospital. I'm sure that pleased Daddy.

I was called down to the office. Minx.

I knocked on his door. He opened it and sat me down on his plush chair which he had already pulled out from behind his desk.

"Ben told me what happened. How are you feeling, Bill?"

Like crap. "I feel fine, Mr. Minx."

"How do you feel, Bill?" He asked again in his toughest vice-principal tone.

"Like crap."

"Ben told me to keep this thing wrapped up tight. I haven't told anyone."

He sat on the edge of his desk.

"Look, I totally misjudged you from the start. The fight with Rick."

I didn't know where this was heading so I just kept quiet. Besides, talking hurt.

"I thought you were on a path to being some sort of bully. And, I always come down hard on fights."

He looked away and his jaw clenched tight.

"I have to explain. But to explain, I have to share something with you."

He stared out his window and continued talking, though softly like he was far away.

"In college I was bullied. I mean seriously bullied. It ended with this guy beating my face to a bloody pulp. I was in the hospital for over a month. Reconstructive surgery."

So, his face had changed since high school. Not as a criminal, but as a victim. He looked back at me.

"I had lots of time to think. Just think. I figured I could either live with hate or try to solve the problem. So, I decided to go into teaching and then administration to head off these bullies before they hurt others."

"So I come down hard on fights. But, I was unjustly hard on you. I'm sorry."

What do you say to that? Especially when saying anything causes you to wince. I just stared at him, keeping as still as possible.

He got up off the desk and I figured the interview was over, so I slowly rose from the chair, wincing. When I looked up at Minx, he was frowning.

"You sure you don't want to rest at home, Bill?"

I smiled. "I'd be hurting there, just as much, Mr. Minx."

He walked me to the door. "How's your granddad doing?"

I stopped and turned.

"How do you know about my granddad?"

"When I first moved to Conaroga, I bought a house right behind his property. Met your granddad on a walk. I could tell he was having memory problems. Helped him out when he let me. Then I guess the memory worked against him and he got suspicious of me. So, I stopped visiting him; I didn't want to add to his problems."

"Hmm..." I murmured thinking. Minx had misjudged me. But, I had misjudged him just as much.

"He's doing fine, sir. Thanks for to helping him when you could."

He patted me on the back as I left. My eyes closed in pain, but I don't think he saw it. Then he closed the door. The hallway was clear. I limped back to class.

As the day wore on, it continued to feel like a million different pains were competing to be that one, serious 'ouch' spot. Soon, however, my physical and emotional pain was channeled into righteous indignation. I didn't do anything wrong. There is no reason I shouldn't at least find out how Sarah was doing in the hospital. When the ending bell sounded, I had decided it was time to see Sarah whether her father liked it or not.

By the time I walked out of school toward the bus, I had figured out how to convince Mom to take me to the hospital. Then I saw Jerry who waved at me and beside him, in uniform, his father, Officer Benjamin Smith.

CHAPTER THIRTY-TWO

"Hi, Billy. Thought I would stop by and drive you boys home."

My eyebrows pressed down and I looked at him slightly sideways. "Everything okay?"

"No, no. Nothing wrong. Just a friendly ride." My stomach began the tumbles again. This was no coincidence.

Jerry, for once, was quiet. He looked straight ahead and just listened. The last twenty-four hours had been a bit strange for him.

Ben looked over at me once we got on the main road.

"Billy, how was school?"

"Little stiff and sore, but otherwise it was all right."

"Sarah is still in the hospital."

"Yeah, I figured as much."

We dropped Jerry off first and then he drove up the hill toward the cabin. About halfway up, Ben pulled over. He stared at me for a few moments. I looked away, knowing what was coming.

"Got a bit of a problem with your neighbor, Kenny Songor."

"Oh?"

"Yeah. Found him dead this morning. Wasn't pretty. You know anything about that?"

I looked out the window away from Mr. Smith. Did I know anything? Yeah, a few things. "I don't know how he died."

I turned back to meet his stare. But the secrets I held were too heavy for my brain so my head slumped downward.

"You made a call from my cell phone, Bill. Number in Rochester. Unlisted, but easy to track. Save me the time and tell me who you called."

Accessory to murder. Now add possible jail time to my miserable life. I closed my eyes and sighed. It was confession time. I met his gaze again and started talking quickly so I would have it all out before I made any more poor decisions.

"Kenny Songor was Al Moreno. Mafia guy. He was the mastermind of the Brinks' robbery back in 1992. During the heist, Al Moreno killed the brother of Robert Salvatore, mafia leader. Mr. Salvatore knew of our interest in the robbery and talked to Sarah and me. He asked me to let him know if ever I ran into Al Moreno. Last night, in the cave, we found three million dollars from the robbery. Al Moreno followed us to the gorge. After we brought the money up from the cave, he was waiting for us with a gun. He killed Jeb Mysurki and Hank Patterson. He was going to shoot us, too, but I talked him into letting us go down the rope. That's how we ended up in the cave. He took the money."

I took a deep breath and resumed. "He cut the rope while we were going back down into the cave. He really wanted us dead, Mr. Smith. Anyway, when you were upstairs, I called Mr. Salvatore and told him what I knew."

Finished with the short explanation, a month of mystery, murder, and mayhem condensed in a minute, I looked away one more time, my heart pounding. How many laws had I broken, I wondered? Would I be put in handcuffs when he took me to the police station in the village? With my luck a picture of me in handcuffs would make the next edition of the paper. What about a lawyer? I didn't think Mr. Seeley would be a good choice.

The silence between us was like a wall and it was pressing ever closer to me. I was starting to breathe heavily. Finally Mr. Smith spoke. "Well, you certainly got around to meet some interesting characters, young man. Salvatore, huh? He's a bigwig in Rochester."

I turned to look at him, ready to put my hands out for the cuffs.

"I've been on the phone with Attorney Seeley."

Oh, wonderful. I moved my hands to my knees.

"And Lieutenant Russell, my boss." So my infractions have gone up the chain of command. Thanks, Ben. I started to move my hands toward him, but dropped them when he continued.

"This is a tricky situation, Billy. We all knew it had something to do with the robbery. Sarah told us that much. But, the less folks know about her and your involvement, the better. So, it was just a dangerous date. Okay?"

I looked at him. Wow. If he had asked me to jump out of the car, take off my shirt and sing the national anthem, I would have said yes. I nodded, feeling lighter than a dandelion puff in soft breeze.

"I didn't tell anyone about the phone call you made last night. My advice is not to tell anyone except maybe your Mom, all right?"

"I'll tell her and no one else, Mr. Smith."

He turned back to me. "Be sure you don't. It would get us both into trouble."

243

He looked straight ahead, held his breath a moment and blew out some air. He was risking his career by not telling anyone my involvement.

"Thanks, Ben."

He flicked his hand at me as though he was swatting an annoying fly, but I could tell it really bothered him.

"It's the right thing for me to do, Billy."

He started the car. He looked over to me, hands gripping and ungripping the steering wheel.

"Sometimes doing the right thing is not always the easiest thing."

I nodded my agreement. This had been a recurring theme for me.

We pulled out onto the road.

"And Billy, there are three dead bodies presently under investigation in Conaroga. We don't have the manpower to figure out just one of these murders, let alone three. Can I have your word you will stop this snooping around? Lieutenant Russell and I can't handle any more dead bodies."

I smiled at him. "Yeah, trust me Mr. Smith. No more detective work from me."

Now that my mind was released from the prospect of jail, I considered the other matter pressing on me. "Ahh. Could I ask you a favor?"

"Sure."

"Could you drive me to the hospital? There's someone I have to talk to." He smiled and started toward the highway.

I called Mom on Ben's phone and told her I had some unfinished business in the city and she understood.

"Tell, Ben, thanks."

"I did, Mom."

"I mean thanks, from me."

I couldn't help myself. "I think you have far better ways of thanking him." Then I hung up.

He looked over at me. His face was colored a bit red, but it still held a smile.

When we got to the hospital, I gingerly got out and then somehow leaned back into the car. "I don't know how long this will take, Mr. Smith."

"Take as long as you want, I'm on the clock."

I turned and walked toward the door. My whole body was hurt but I didn't want anyone to see me limp. I was angry. Once inside the hospital, I walked purposefully toward the elevator. Alone in the metal box my face screwed up with pain when it jerked up. Out of the elevator, I walked steadily toward Sarah's door. I went to open it and Rick Henson came out.

CHAPTER THIRTY-THREE

Rick was momentarily startled by me. After he looked me up and down, he smiled and said, "Hey, Billy. You look like crap."

"Hey, Rick. Great picture in the papers."

The smile got bigger. "Yeah, how about that? Didn't mean to upstage you. I know what you did, dude. You are something fierce, Bill."

"Hmm…"

He looked back at the door and then put his hand on my shoulder. "Don't worry about Sarah and me. She really likes you." Rick smiled and jauntily walked down the hall. He seemed far too smug for my liking. Just as my hand reached the doorknob, the door opened again, pushing me back. Boy, did that hurt. Even though I was trying to be stoic, I gasped out an "Ouch." When I looked up at the culprit I was face to face with Mr. Seeley.

He stared at me. I gulped. This was going to be harder than I thought. Nevertheless, I was determined to see Sarah. "Mr. Seeley, I know you told me to stay away, but I can't do that. I have to find out how Sarah's doing and…"

"Wait a second, Taylor." He closed the door and looked back at me with a face which seemed to have aged ten years since I last saw him. He grabbed my arm (somehow I refrained from wincing) and led me away from the door.

"Look. I was wrong last night. Sarah filled me in on some details. Then I found out how dangerous it was. I, well, I…" He looked away, his whole face a rock, except for his eyes that were blinking. He looked back at me as though seeing me for the first time. The tightness from his face lifted as he scrutinized me.

"Billy, you look like crap."

"So, I've been told."

Mr. Seeley put his hand on my shoulder. That hurt and I must have finally given in to the pain because he quickly took it off.

"What I'm trying to say is that I was wrong about you, young man."

He looked away a moment.

"I would have lost my daughter if it hadn't been for you," he whispered.

When he looked at me again there were tears in his eyes. "Thanks, Billy for what you did."

His voice choked and then he finished. "I'll never forget it." He looked down at the ground a moment, turned and followed Rick.

Well, I thought, got by the dragon fairly easily. Now, for the princess. I opened the door and stuck my head in.

She was sitting up in the bed, watching some talk show on television. Sarah looked tired, but absolutely beautiful. She saw me at the door and beamed a great smile. This time the sun miraculously peaked from behind a cloud and actually did make the room brighter. The smile helped though.

"I was wondering when you might get here."

"I was here last night but your father kinda discouraged me from coming in."

She scowled. "I talked to him about that." She reached for the remote and turned off the TV.

"I told him what happened." She was connected with at least a half dozen wires and tubes while her right arm was carried in a sling. "I also told him that pretty much everything was my idea, and I pushed you into things."

Then she looked up at me, angry. "You still could have snuck past him last night or called at least!"

"I mean your dad pushed me out and I saw you holding Rick's hand last night and I thought…"

She looked at me sternly. "You thought what? That I was getting back together with him? Really, Billy."

"He carried you out and got you to the ambulance," I said.

"And you and I both know what you did, Billy. You risked your life to save mine. Any longer and I might have lost my arm, you know."

She tilted her head, eyebrows knitted in confusion. "Hey, when we were going back up the cliff, did you bite me?"

I winced. "Yeah, but I had kinda had to. You were slipping out. Had to wake you."

She thought about my answer for a moment. "Well, okay. But don't bite me anymore. Understood?"

"Last bite. I promise you."

"And what are you doing by the door?" she demanded.

"You know, I mean… I don't know."

Carefully adjusting her wires and tubes, she scooted over to make room on her bed and patted right beside her. "Get over here before I start to cry. I want you here beside me. Not Rick or anyone else. You."

I walked over to her, winced once, and looked up at a concerned face. She held her good arm to me and I leaned into her. I estimated by that time in my life I had about thirty kisses from all my girlfriends. I didn't count the nearly one hundred Sheryl Shoemaker gave me in fourth grade. And, to be honest, ten of the thirty kisses were from Sarah, but usually on the cheek or a quick peck on the lips. I had better kisses from some girls in Florida. One was a French kiss and that confused me. But... this kiss. Wow. It blew them all, together, out of the water. It seemed to last forever, but probably only a few seconds.

The rollercoaster ride was pretty good about then.

There was a knock on the door. Maude Patterson peaked her head in. "May we come in?" Sarah waved her in with her good hand as I started to get off the bed. Sarah yanked me back down. Maude was followed by a sheepish Tom.

After assuring her friend she was all right, Sarah gave a brief description of what happened. Mrs. Patterson looked at me.

"I thought you were special when I met you, William. You saved her life, young man. Do you know that?"

"Well... I... ahh."

"Yes, he knows it." Sarah responded, exasperated.

She looked at Sarah. "You are a lucky girl, Miss Seeley."

Sarah squeezed my hand and I yelped. Gently rubbing the top of my hand, she said, "He's my knight in shining armor. But, my knight is a bit sore this afternoon."

I flinched. I was as uncomfortable with all the praise as I was with the pain. I was delighted when Mrs. Patterson changed the focus of our conversation.

"Well, I have a knight in shining armor as well, Miss Sarah." With that she pulled Tom close. He put his arm around her.

"He helped me when the world was pushing down on me so much I thought I would be smothered to death." She didn't go into details, but she was beaming. Today she didn't need any make-up. She was that happy. Sarah was beaming right along with Maude, her romantic vision finally crystalized into reality.

Maude shared how Tom came into her life. Tom even related a story about he was going to surprise her with a picnic when he saw us in the driveway that day we visited her and talked to Hank. The mysterious visit by Tom now explained.

*

When I got back to Ben's car, he drove me over to the police station in town. There I met Joe Russell, Ben's boss. He and Ben interrogated me about nearly everything. It wasn't like I had a bright light shining in my face. Mr. Russell mostly talked about Letchworth Park and how he often engaged in illegal climbs with his friends when he was young. Great stories and he got me laughing a number of times. I felt so relaxed and safe, my experiences of the last few weeks just tumbled out. Then he would interrupt me and tell another story. The only thing I didn't share was the cell phone call. Besides his stories, the only thing that Mr. Russell shared was that the suitcase with the money was missing. Our conclusions, however, were the same. The money at last got to the mafia.

Sarah left the hospital the next day. She told me on the phone that she had to stay home a couple more days. "See you after school tomorrow?" she asked hopefully.

"No, sorry. Gotta watch granddad." Her silence spoke her disappointment. "But, I'll see you early tomorrow morning before school."

I kept my promise. Her house was four miles away. A good morning jog. It took me less than an hour, but there I was knocking on the front door, huffing from my run. Mr. Seeley, wrapped in a bathrobe, opened the door.

"Billy. You're early." He looked at his watch. "It's six-thirty."

"I know. I left home a bit after six."

"You ran here?" Then he stuck his head out the door to look for a car. Looking back at me, he smiled. "You are quite a guy,

251

Mr. Taylor. Sarah's in the kitchen. She thought you might get here early."

So, for an hour we were together, chaperoned by her parents and the cook, Delores, all at different times. I showered in the guest bathroom and Mrs. Seeley drove me to school.

When I got home that afternoon Mom asked how the morning went and I just smiled. She ran to the car and drove off to work. I spent a few minutes with Gramps when I heard the car come back up the driveway. Mom must have forgotten something. I went to the door to find out what she needed. She gets frantic when she doesn't get to work fifteen minutes early. I opened the door and was face to face with Louie, my mafia nemesis. The rollercoaster again.

CHAPTER THIRTY-FOUR

My heart stopped for a moment, then fell into my stomach. He was alone on the porch but there was a black limousine in the driveway with three younger guys standing beside it. One smoking and watching the road, a second one watching me carefully and the third guy was urinating on the flower bed.

Louie wore a black suit, not a crease on it. Waiting to be invited in, he just stood at the door. I wasn't about to let him into my home. His eyes narrowed and his face darkened. I didn't want to anger him either, though. I stepped out onto the porch. He nodded to me slightly as though he acknowledged the gesture on my part.

"Mr. Taylor." He announced formally. "Don Salvatore sends his regards. He also sends his heartfelt thanks. His words."

I didn't know quite what to say. "Uh, tell him thanks. Or, you're welcome."

Louie put his right hand to his chin, his face frowning and looking at the ground. "I think the 'you're welcome' is best." He smiled at me. "He also gives you a present."

I shook my head. "Not necessary. No gifts."

Louie scowled. "Look, you don't say no to this man. Certainly you never turn down a present. You understand?"

My heart was now pumping wildly. "Yes. Thank him for the gift."

He smiled. "Good."

Silence. Louie looked to the side, jaws muscles flexing. Oh God, what now? He looked up at me.

"Mr. Salvatore sent me because I overreacted with you. The last guy I got mad with was an asshole and I... well, no need to go into that. So, I came here to apologize."

He looked at me, frowning. Apparently he found it difficult to apologize.

"Nothing to apologize for, Louie."

His eyes blinked a moment and he looked at me, eyes wide. "Hey, that's what I told Don Salvatore." He patted me on the back.

"You're all right, you know."

Silence. He was looking at me, waiting for a response. "Ahh... thanks."

Silence. He looked sideways and his jaw clenched. Jesus, what was going on? Finally, he turned back to me. "Look, could you do me a favor?"

"Sure." And then please leave!

His face winced as though it hurt to ask for favors. Then he squeezed his eyes shut. When he opened them, there was no uncertainty, no hesitation, but the eyes were angry.

"Show me how you threw me down that day in the restaurant."

If he had asked me to slow dance with him, I would have been less surprised.

"You want me to teach you how to throw somebody?"

"Yeah, that karate shit."

"Judo." I corrected him.

"Judo, karate, kung fu. It's all Chink tricks."

Judo actually originated in Japan, but I didn't correct him. The next ten minutes found a high school student teaching a mafia killer judo.

"Can I try it on you now? Please, William. Those guys, they were there that day."

I sighed. I was still sore from the rock-climbing and the run. But, I didn't want this man resentful in any way.

"All right."

He crouched down. "You come at me now, kid."

I lunged for him and he executed the move I taught him perfectly. I was suddenly flat on the ground and his foot was on my throat.

Above me, with a flat voice, he said, "I learned good, didn't I, kid?"

The shoe was pressing just a little too hard on my Adam's apple and the eyes above me were anything, but friendly. After staring at me a moment more, he removed his shoe and reached a hand out. I took it and he pulled me up.

"I am grateful for the lesson, William. Have a good day." He turned on his heel and jauntily bounced down the steps. His entourage all smiled at him before they got in the car. The smoker flicked the cigarette in the garden and opened the door for Louie. He patted him on the back as he slipped into the car. The engine started up and then they were gone. I waited a minute more, expecting them to return since Louie had forgotten about the gift. Probably would come in the mail.

Finally, I walked into the house and checked on Gramps. As ever, he was busy sorting his change. When I looked back into the hallway by the door, I noticed a suitcase by the closet. It had been cleaned up considerably, but I recognized it. Walking closer I saw the initials PTT embossed by the handle. To this day, I don't know how granddad's suitcase got inside the cabin. But, it was there, the focus of my life these last two months. With shaking hands I gently laid it down on the kitchen table and opened it up. There were neat piles of hundred dollar bills. I looked over my shoulder and saw granddad standing beside me.

"Can I count it, Billy?"

I shut the case and carried it to his table. He sat down and, after twenty years, he patiently waited while I cleared the table of his coins. Then I put the bills out in packets. With trembling hands, he sorted the money. Two perfectly equal stacks formed on opposite ends of the table. As near as I could estimate, Mr. Salvatore had returned the entire amount Sarah and I found in the cave. Salvatore's men must have retrieved it after they killed Mr. Songor... Al Moreno. Grandpa kept arranging and rearranging the piles until he went to bed. I stayed up until Mom got home. Her mouth dropped when she saw the neat piles on Granddad's table. A hand went to her mouth to stifle a scream of delight.

"My God, Billy. Three million dollars! Do you know what we can do with three million? New house, new car, Gramps properly taken care of..."

I had already thought about all those possibilities. I didn't want to get caught up with her giddiness so I interrupted her. "Mom, it has to be returned."

Her head tilted and her eyes squinted. It looked like she was mad so I quickly explained.

"Mom, I was just thinking about what Dad said once. I lied to him about breaking one of his tools. His drill. It was when I was building that tree house. Burned out the motor. Anyway, he figured it out. He didn't spank me, Mom. He just sat me down and talked to me. He said a lie looks like a rope that will save you, but it really is a noose ready to hang you. I think this money is the same thing. We would have to hide it. But once we started hiding it, the problem would grow. The right thing is to give it back. It's really not ours, anyway. I think that's what Dad would have done."

She looked at me as tears filled her eyes. "Yes, he would have done just that. And, I'm proud his son is just like him."

She looked back at the pile of green packets. "So, what do we do now?"

I thought a moment. "I don't know, but Ben might."

The next day was a blur to me. Mr. Smith and Mom talked in the morning. The Brink's people arrived in the afternoon with Lieutenant Russell. The story was slowly unveiled for the officials.

After I told them how Louie dropped off the money, the adults just stared at me, all silent for an entire minute. Finally, Ben broke the silence. "Gentlemen, this could get messy. Mafia and money, even when they give it back, can be a dangerous combination. I think we keep this whole thing secret."

They all looked at me again. I breathed out a great sigh of relief and my shoulders relaxed. "Mr. Smith is right. Please, keep it secret."

The three Brinks' personnel and Mr. Russell went into the kitchen and chatted a bit.

When they returned, Lieutenant Russell spoke. "We have to make an announcement about the money, Billy and it's been my experience that the truth is always the best way to go."

I slumped. Who knew where this notoriety might take me.

"So we are going to say the money was returned by a citizen who desires to stay anonymous. Nothing about the mob, the cave, or the murders."

A great sigh of relief and I thanked the men. They left with the three million dollars. End result? I had one terrific girlfriend, a number of new friends (including Rick Henson), Mom found someone to hang out with and, well, I guess it was all worth it.

CHAPTER THIRTY-FIVE

Rick Henson led the Blue Devils to one victory after another all the way to the sectional championship, and the "Hero of the Gorge" became a favorite of the local papers. I didn't mind the anonymity since I had Sarah as my girlfriend.

About three weeks after returning the money, I got a letter of appreciation from the CEO of Brinks. He said some nice things about me and I almost missed the last sentence.

"The reward money shall be sent to you within the next few days."

I smiled. Reward money. Sarah thought it would have to be a few thousand. I just laughed. More like a few hundred. She was so naïve sometimes.

"Maybe," I replied, not wanting to disappoint her. "If so, how about I take you to the Oakdale Inn?"

She liked the idea and I was pretty sure we could afford that.

Saturday morning Mom brought the mail in. She waived a certified envelope at me, smiled, and opened it. Slowly chewing some toast, I watched her read it once, hold up the check, get her glasses on, and looked at the check again. She slowly sat down, trembling hands to her mouth. I grabbed the letter. I saw the check. $3000.00. Well, not too bad. Sarah was right again.

Then I looked more closely, there was no decimal point. The check was for three hundred thousand dollars, 10% of the money found. Mom had been watching me. When I looked at her she grabbed my hand and cried.

So, I took Sarah out to a really nice restaurant in Rochester. No Oakdale Inn for this couple. I drove, having just passed my driving test. After a tasty, but rather skimpy dinner (personally you get a better bargain at the local Wendy's), we had a rather heated kissing session in the van, the details of which I don't intend to share with anyone.

Mom paid off Dad's debt, we got a car for me, and put in a heating system for the cabin.

Granddad was our main concern. He was slipping deeper into the black pool called Alzheimer's disease. We were advised to get help from the Alzheimer's Association in Rochester. They guided us through the maze of health and financial issues. With their guidance we put Gramps in a relatively inexpensive day care. The money, as much as it was, disappeared like the white fluff of a dandelion in a strong wind. Though I still cared for him in the evenings, I was able to join the track team in the spring. I won sectionals for the mile and went to the State finals. I didn't win, but I placed second. For Bill Taylor, junior at Coneroga High School, life was good.

Then the rollercoaster started up again.

CHAPTER THIRTY-SIX

It was a classic early June Saturday in Coneroga… not a cloud in the sky and temperatures reaching into the seventies. A perfect day for a picnic which was what my friends and I were going to do that afternoon. There was a knock on the door and I whistled the latest tune from a romantic comedy Sarah and I saw the night before. Louie stared at me from the other side of the screen.

"William."

"Louie."

He had changed. There were worry lines on his face and the easy smile had disappeared. It wasn't that he was frowning. He was just looking, well serious.

"I have a favor to ask."

I tilted my head warily. Ahh, so here it comes. They do me good with the money and they expect something in return. It was all scripted in the Godfather movies.

"What's the favor?" I asked stepping onto the porch.

I wasn't sure, but I think his eyes were glistening a bit. "Mr. Salvatore is in the hospital and I'm sure he would like to see you."

Why would Mr. Salvatore want to see me? It didn't matter. Don't ask me why or even how, but I had affection for the old man. I turned back to Louie. "Wait here."

I talked briefly to Mom and went with Louie in his limousine. Smoker was driving. He said nothing. We sat in spotless leather seats in the back. "Thanks for doing this, William. It will mean a lot to him."

"What's wrong?"

"Congestive heart failure. He's seventy-six, two bullet wounds, and a heart attack ten years ago. But now I see him very weak, William, very weak." He looked away.

We were at the same hospital Sarah stayed at nearly a year before. When we got to Mr. Salvatore's suite, two of his soldiers were stationed outside the door. One of them opened the door for Louie.

"Robert, I have a friend to see you."

Mr. Salvatore had an oxygen mask on and looked frail in the large bed, various wires connected to his body. He motioned me to his bedside with a crook of his finger. He wheezed out a few words. "Sit down, William."

Watery eyes stared at me.

"I want to talk alone to Mr. Taylor."

Louie nodded and then walked out.

His breathing was steady, but labored. He asked about the details of what happened in the cave. When I was done, he first inquired about Sarah.

"She's doing fine, sir. Total recovery."

"Good that you called me, William. The bastard would have gotten away otherwise."

I nodded while he rested from the exertion of talking.

"Louie tells me you spent the money on your grandfather."

"Most of it. Some went to improvement in our home."

He smiled. "It's good you think of it as home, William. Last time you kept calling it a house."

He closed his eyes and I thought for a moment he was sleeping. Then with his eyes shut, he asked another question. "Why didn't you keep all the money, William?"

"Because it wasn't mine, Mr. Salvatore."

His eyes remained closed. "We all make choices, William. When I was your age, I saw this guy murder someone. I said nothing."

He paused a moment, breathing hard. His eyes opened, he looked at me and continued.

"A few days later the same man gave me some money. Who am I to refuse such a gift? My decision to keep quiet... well, it took me down my path." Don Salvatore stared at me and I nodded. His eyes closed again. "Louie runs the business now. Not always smart, but dependable. And he listens to me."

I understood the gravitas Louie had assumed.

Mr. Salvatore chuckled and then coughed. When he gained control, he hissed out more words: "So many circles, William. Louie's father was the man who gave me the hundred dollars for keeping quiet. Now I give Louie a business worth hundreds of millions. Funny, huh?"

I smiled at him. He looked away for a moment and then turned back to me.

"William, I'm tired now."

He reached out his hand and I held it. His grip started strong. Then it relaxed as his breathing became more steady and deep. Mr. Salvatore was sleeping.

*

A week later I got a phone call from Louie. Robert Salvatore died peaceably at home in his sleep. I decided to go to the funeral. Sarah wanted to go, but her father pointed out that the press would have considerable grist for the rumor mill if the daughter of a rising attorney's attended. I agreed with him and, miracle of miracles, Sarah begrudgingly conceded.

Mom refused to have me go alone. So she drove me but stayed outside the ring of cars that surrounded the cemetery. Nevertheless she was photographed a number of times as was I. Apparently the papers and the government were both interested in the proceedings.

Louie greeted me with a solemn handshake. "I am grateful to you for coming, William. You being here… well, it says something about you. I won't forget it."

I nodded and he led me to the inner ring of people. Mrs. Salvatore, a little, round lady, white hair sneaking out under her shawl, stood stoically beside her son, Johnny. There were no tears. Death was not a stranger to this family.

After the prayer and the ceremonial tossing of handfuls of dirt on the coffin, I gave my condolences to her.

She grabbed my hand. "Yes, I know you. Robert, he talked of you. You threw Louie to the ground." She winked at Louie who was at her side. He shrugged. There was no anger in his face.

"He said you were a good boy."

"I will miss him, Mrs. Salvatore." She looked to the ground and nodded. Then someone else vied for her attention and I excused myself. A chapter in my life had been closed. Or, so I thought.

*

My Dad graduated from St. Lawrence University, so I had always hoped to follow in his footsteps. Ironically, the boon from the reward money went down in the books as our family having an extra three hundred thousand dollars and I was denied the scholarship which I would have otherwise been entitled. The old adage comes to mind: no good deed goes unpunished. So I resigned myself to attending the local college, Conaroga State University. A good school to be sure, but not St. Lawrence. We could spare a few dollars from the left over funds, but I would have to work part time to cover other expenses. Mom and I both knew we might have to take out a loan, but it would be manageable.

Now I was in my senior year, running cross country. One autumn Saturday morning, I heard a scream from my mom. I ran to her. She had just picked up the mail. She was holding a letter in one trembling hand, her other hand held to her lips.

"What's wrong, Mom?"

"Oh, Billy." And she handed me the letter.

The letter head was from American Made, the clothing business which was the vanguard of Mr. Salvatore's entirely legitimate business endeavor. The letter started with the word, "Congratulations." Apparently I was the first recipient of the Robert L. Salvatore scholarship. Full ride to any college of my choice with spending money of ten thousand dollars for books and incidentals. For this largesse from the Salvatore family, I was required to work summers with the company at the hefty salary of twenty thousand dollars. I wondered how much of this was orchestrated by Louie.

I was left with a dilemma. Did I really want to be indebted to them? In the back of mind were Ben's words about doing the right thing, not the easy thing. My father had said much the same thing. This was still indirectly accepting money from the mob. I explained my concerns to Mom. She angrily refuted them, and then I got defensive and countered with my knowledge of how the mafia worked.

Sarah came over that night for dinner and the three of us discussed the offer. After both women gave lengthy explanations why I should accept the scholarship, there was silence. I had already made up my mind.

"So, are you going to accept it, Billy?" Sarah asked.

"It's still a gift from the mafia." I started.

They simultaneously reiterated arguments to excuse such a connection.

I held my hand up to silence them. Then, I shrugged my shoulders the way Mr. Salvatore had done over a year ago when I first met him. In a raspy voice I said: "Who am I to refuse such a gift?"

*

THE END

Dear Reader:

"The Runner and The Robber" has a fascinating plot and, though a work of fiction, the caregiver experience it features is real.

At the Alzheimer's Association, we hear many challenging personal stories about people becoming caregivers for a family member or friend with Alzheimer's disease. An increasing number of those stories involve young people caring for grandparents and doing so with commitment.

Across the country, there are an estimated 15 million dementia caregivers. About 10 percent of them are younger than 35, and a growing number of families with children at home are providing care for loved ones with dementia. These caregivers give up more than time. They give up jobs, promotions, opportunities and passions. They face emotional and physical strain to ensure the safety, well-being and dignity of their loved ones.

The Alzheimer's Association provides support groups, education, respite care and resources for caregivers. Our mission is to eliminate Alzheimer's disease through the advancement of research; to provide and enhance care for all affected; and to reduce the risk of dementia through the promotion of brain health.

Caregivers need your support and understanding, too. To learn more about Alzheimer's, dementia and how you can help, please visit **www.alz.org**.

Teresa A. Galbier
President/CEO
Alzheimer's Association Rochester & Finger Lakes Region
Rochester, NY

Dear Reader

Like many of you, someone I love has Alzheimer's disease. It's been heartbreaking to watch as the disease progressively robs him of his memory, and, likewise, it's been extremely difficult to witness the toll it has taken on his wife—his main caregiver of many years. She's had to learn how to not only provide care, but, also, take care of herself and ask for help when she needs it.

Across the country, there are an estimated 15 million dementia caregivers. *The Runner and The Robber* tells the story of a young caregiver. More than 15 percent of caregivers are younger than 35 and there's a growing number of caregivers who are already caring for children while providing care for a family member with dementia. These caregivers are the very definition of 'selfless' and give up much of their academic, career and personal goals in order to care for a loved one.

Theirs is often a silent struggle, but it doesn't have to be. With support, caregivers can learn to speak up about their needs and, hopefully, find a community willing to listen. That's among the many things the Alzheimer's Association does. Support groups, education, respite care and more are among the many services the Alzheimer's Association offers. It's been beneficial to my family in ways I can't adequately describe. To learn more about Alzheimer's, dementia and how the organization can help you, visit **www.alz.org**.

Norma Holland
Anchor/Reporter
13WHAM News
Rochester, New York

The Runner and the Robber was loosely based on an infamous Brinks' robbery. Some parts, like the statement about the truck being stolen at a Dunkin Donuts, were borrowed from similar heists in the same city.

On Jan. 5, 1993, three masked gunmen entered the Brinks Co. depot, just outside downtown Rochester. With a sagging fence and a building peeling with paint, the facility did not resemble a financial nexus where millions were brought in and sent out in Brinks' trucks every day. The anonymity of the place may have been the reason security was so lax. Unfortunately, someone who worked there saw an opportunity for robbery.

One of the few guards, a retired Rochester police Officer Thomas O'Connor, already had a checkered past. He had connections with the Irish Republican Army. It was known by authorities that he smuggled a former IRA rebel and friend, Samuel Millar, into the United States.

The crime itself was relatively straight forward. A few masked men walked through a hole in the fence and, right before the money was to be transferred to various Brinks' trucks, personnel were held up and over seven million dollars was stolen.

During the celebrated heist, O'Connor was kidnapped during the crime. In fact, he was the only employee kidnapped. He was later released unharmed. Some law enforcement officers viewed this as a ruse to deflect suspicions away from him.

One of the many suspects was Samuel Millar, the same IRA rebel who O'Connor brought into the country. He was found living in New Jersey and, for months after the heist, was watched by the local police. When detectives finally decided it was time for a search warrant, nearly $2 million of the missing money was recovered from a hiding place in Millar's home. Documents with the cash connected Millar to the Rev. Patrick Moloney, a

Catholic priest who also a friend of the IRA. In November 1993 the FBI arrested O'Connor, Moloney, and Millar. Five million dollars were missing and, in fact, are still missing today.

In 1994 a jury convicted Moloney and Millar while O'Connor was acquitted.

Millar claimed that he and another man, a former boxer Ronnie Gibbons, came up with the plan. There was no proof that Gibbons was directly connected with the robbery but he may have been involved with the missing five million. Millar stated that the money was originally intended for the IRA when another man, perhaps Gibbons, intercepted the money.

In 1995 Gibbons mysteriously disappeared. The lower half of his body was discovered in 2012 and identified by DNA. There is no convincing evidence that the IRA ever got any money from the heist. It is possible Gibbons may have hid the money before he was murdered. Perhaps he gave it to a park ranger for safe-keeping.

ABOUT THE AUTHOR

Robert Sells has taught physics for over forty years. He has been a story teller for over fifty years, entertaining his children, grandchildren, and students.

The *Return of the White Deer* is his first offering to the public. His second novel *Reap The Whirlwind* was released late summer 2013.

He lives with his wife, Dale, in the idyllic village of Geneseo, New York with two attentive dogs who are uncritical sounding boards for his new stories. He is intrigued by poker and history, in love with Disney and writing, and amused by religion and politics.

935R00151

Made in the USA
Columbia, SC
08 October 2017